DOCTOR WHO

2 new adventures

Also available:

Death Riders by Justin Richards

Heart of Stone by Trevor Baxendale

The Good, the Bad and the Alien
by Colin Brake

System Wipe by Oli Smith

Alien Adventures

by Richard Dinnick and Mike Tucker

Sightseeing in Space

by David Bailey and Steve Lyons

Monstrous Missions

by Gary Russell and Jonathan Green

Want to get closer to the Doctor
and learn more about the very best
Doctor Who books out there?

Go to
www.doctorwhochildrensbooks.co.uk
for news, reviews, competitions
and more!

BBC Children's Books
Published by the Penguin Group
Penguin Books Ltd, 80 Strand, London, WC2R 0RL, England
Penguin Group (USA) Inc., 375 Hudson Street, New York 10014, USA
Penguin Books (Australia) Ltd, 250 Camberwell Road, Camberwell,
Victoria 3124, Australia (A division of Pearson Australia Group PTY Ltd)
Penguin Group (NZ), 67 Apollo Drive, Rosedale, North Shore
0632, New Zealand (A division of Pearson New Zealand Ltd)
Canada, India, South Africa
Published by BBC Children's Books, 2012

Extra Time written by Richard Dungworth
The Water Thief written by Jacqueline Rayner
Cover illustrated by Kev Walker and Paul Campbell

001 – 10 9 8 7 6 5 4 3 2 1

ISBN – 978-14059-0-805-4

Printed in Great Britain by Clays Ltd, St Ives plc

STEP BACK IN TIME

RICHARD DUNGWORTH
JACQUELINE RAYNER

CONTENTS

DOCTOR WHO

EXTRA TIME

RICHARD DUNGWORTH

CHAPTER 1
ON THE BEAT

Police Constable Sanderson was feeling rather sorry for himself.

He stood on the corner of Fulton Road and watched the parade of excited football fans pass noisily by. There was a steady stream of people moving south along the straight, broad route of Olympic Way. Others were making their way from Wembley Park Underground station, or spilling out of bright red double-decker buses on the Fulton Road, to join the flow. It was as if everyone in north-west London was being drawn to the same spot by some irresistible force.

Everyone except me, thought PC Sanderson glumly.

The disappointed policeman knew only too well where the crowd was heading. Olympic Way led directly to the main entrance of Wembley Stadium. The home of football. And today, for the first time ever, the scene of the FIFA World Cup Final.

There was little doubt who most fans had come to support. The cross of St George and the Union Jack were everywhere PC Sanderson looked – on flags, banners, clothing and faces. The air was full of patriotic chanting, excited chatter and the *tatta-tatta-tatta* of the fans' wooden football rattles. Men, women and children, of all ages and backgrounds, had come to cheer on their nation's heroes of the hour.

The young constable had seen big Wembley crowds before. He had once been on duty on FA Cup Final day. But he had never seen anything quite like this.

However, there had never been a match quite like this. A World Cup Final, at Wembley, with the home side contending for the trophy. It was the stuff of every English fan's dreams.

And PC Sanderson was going to miss the whole thing.

Trust my rotten luck, thought Sanderson miserably. *Only I could get the Saturday shift, today of all days...*

He gave a weary sigh as he watched yet more excited England fans flood past. Right now, the rest of his family would be gathered in his neighbour's front room, watching the pre-match build-up. And here *he* was, stuck on the beat, and not due to clock off until several hours after the final whistle.

Maybe a cuppa would lift his spirits. It was a sunny July afternoon, and under his black bobby's hat and uniform, Sanderson was feeling the heat. It was surprising how thirst-quenching a nice cup of tea could be, even on a summer's day.

He turned away from the flow of fans, and began strolling back towards the junction with Albion Way. He had stashed his thermos flask in the police call box there. It was common practice for Met officers on the beat to use the nearest box as a base. Its direct phone line to the local station gave an on-duty officer a useful link with headquarters. The large, dark blue, wardrobe-like boxes had been introduced to London's streets a little over thirty years ago. There were now over six hundred dotted around the city – including the one on Albion Way.

'Do you reckon the lads can win it for us, officer?'

Sanderson broke his stride at the sound of a familiar cheerful voice. Syd Marlin, a newspaper seller who was a Fulton Road regular, was hailing him from his stand on the opposite side of the street. At least *someone* else was working, then.

Sanderson crossed the road. Syd was always up for a chat.

'They'll have their work cut out, Syd, that's for sure,' the policeman said as he approached the news-stand. 'The Germans have some quality players. Beckenbauer, Seeler, Emmerich – they all know how to put the ball in the net. But I'd like to think we'll give 'em a game.'

'Never thought we'd make it this far, misself,' said Syd. 'What with young Jimmy Greaves out injured, an' all. Thought Portugal would do for us in the semi. But Ramsey's turning out to be quite some manager, ain't 'e? Played a blinder so far. And there ain't a better number nine in the world than Charlton, by my reckoning.'

'We've got the talent, all right,' agreed Sanderson. 'Let's hope Lady Luck is on our side. I guess we just have to keep faith, eh, Syd?'

PC Sanderson stepped off the pavement briefly to allow a party of young men and women to pass by. They, too, were heading for Olympic Way. All were dressed in the very latest fashion.

Syd watched the group of youngsters move off along the street. He shook his head and tutted.

'Look at 'em, officer,' he muttered. 'Right bunch of peacocks, these young 'uns, ain't they? My missis don't approve of them new "miniskirts". Says they're not decent.'

Sanderson raised his eyebrows beneath his police helmet. 'Well, they're certainly all the rage this summer, that's for sure,' he said.

Syd nodded.

'Aye. There was a real pretty redhead along just a minute ago, wearing one,' he said. 'Stopped off to buy a paper, she did – or rather, one of the two blokes with her did.' He hesitated, frowning. 'Funniest thing, though. Not one of the three of 'em seemed to have the faintest idea 'ow to pay for it.' He shook his head again. 'Not a clue.'

PC Sanderson gave the vendor a puzzled look.

'How d'you mean, Syd?'

'Just what I say. They didn't know 'ow to pay. The one who wanted the paper took out a whole 'andful of coins, and just stared at them, like 'e 'ad no idea which ones to give me. His mate wanted a few of them penny bubblegum specials.'

He pointed at a cardboard tray of sweets at one side of his stand. Their green, black and white wrappers bore the words "Bazooka World Cup Footballers".

'With three of them, and the paper,' Syd went on, 'it came to sixpence. But when I asked the fella with the money for a tanner, 'e jus' looked at me like I was talking gibberish. Then he gave me a whole half crown – five times what he owed! And 'e wouldn't have anything back from me – tho' I tried to give 'im 'is change, I swear.'

'Foreigners, maybe?' suggested Sanderson.

'That's what I thought,' replied Syd. 'But both blokes spoke to me in the Queen's English. And the lass was Scottish, clear as day – which is 'ardly proper foreign…'

A transistor radio – the small, portable type that almost everyone seemed to own these days – stood on a shelf at the back of Syd's news-stand. A recent Beatles hit had been playing in the background. Now a new track began, with a burst of raucous, angry-sounding vocals. It was The Who, blaring out their hit, "My Generation". Syd reached for the radio's tuning dial, and cut the up-and-coming band off.

'That's enough of that racket. I don't make much of this stuff the kids are all listening to now. "Mods", they call 'emselves, don't they?

Not enough tune for my liking. I know it's "in", of course. But I never was one for all that fashion malarkey.'

PC Sanderson smiled. 'Nor me, Syd.'

'My eldest is *right* into it, though,' Syd went on. He twiddled the radio's tuning dial, trying to pick up another station. 'Got 'imself one of them Italian motor scooters, an' everythin'. Wing mirrors all over the thing…'

Suddenly the crackle of radio static was replaced by the sound of a well-spoken male voice.

'*…and the stands here at Wembley are rapidly filling with England's expectant supporters. The atmosphere is truly electric. One can only wonder how Alf Ramsey's players are feeling at this moment, as they prepare themselves in the south-side changing rooms for this historic encounter…*'

'Not long till kick-off now,' said Syd. 'I'd best get a move on. My sister's old man managed to pick up a second-hand televisual set, on the cheap. I'm off to watch the match at her place. How about you, officer? I guess you're knocking off, too?'

'Afraid not, Syd. I was just going to grab a cuppa. I'm on duty all afternoon – more's the pity.'

The newspaper seller looked horrified.

'No! You're missing the match?' he hissed. 'A game like this only comes round once in a lifetime – if you're lucky. It ain't right to miss it!'

'I know, Syd. I can't pretend I'm happy about it.'

Syd frowned. He appeared to think hard about something for a few moments.

'Here.' He lifted the still-chattering wireless, and presented it to PC Sanderson. 'You take this, my friend. You can tuck it away in that police box of yours. Have yourself a little listen to how Ramsey's lads are getting on.'

Sanderson shook his head. 'That's very good of you, Syd, but I can't,' he said regretfully. 'Not when I'm supposed to be on duty.'

'Who's to know?' pressed Syd, still holding out the radio. 'You can give it me back when you get the chance.'

The constable dithered.

'Go on with yer! It's the World Cup Final, for

Pete's sake! I'll not tell a soul.'

Sanderson gave a sigh. 'Ah, why not? You're right – it might not come round again for a while, eh?' He took the wireless, and tucked it under his arm. 'Thanks, Syd. You're a gent.'

Syd grinned.

'No problem, officer. Now, I best shut up shop, or I'll miss the start misself.'

PC Sanderson gave another nod of thanks. Then, leaving Syd to close up his news-stand, he set off along the pavement once again. This time, there was real purpose in his stride.

A hundred paces or so brought him to the junction with Albion Way. He turned the corner briskly – and came to an abrupt halt.

Now that was odd. *Very* odd.

It was only just over an hour since Sanderson had last called at the Albion Way box – to park his police motorcycle beside it, and drop off his flask.

But within that time, there had been a very obvious change on Albion Way.

There were now *two* police boxes.

They stood right next to one another, and were

more or less identical.

PC Sanderson was baffled. The second box must somehow have been put in position during the last hour. But how? And, more to the point, *why*? There were no plans to replace the existing box, as far as he was aware. Certainly nothing had been mentioned at the station. Besides, the newly arrived box looked in worse condition, if anything, than the original one.

The obvious thing to do was to phone in, and find out what was going on. But Sanderson found himself hesitating. He looked at Syd's radio tucked under his arm. Now that he had a chance to enjoy at least some of the England-West Germany game, he was reluctant to draw attention to himself for the next couple of hours.

There would be plenty of time to sort out whatever the muddle was afterwards.

Having made up his mind, he opened the door of the familiar police box, stepped inside, and closed it behind him.

CHAPTER 2
THE ROAD TO WEMBLEY

'Yessss! Brilliant!' said Rory. 'I got Gordon Banks!'

Rory, Amy and the Doctor were being swept along Olympic Way by the tide of people heading for Wembley. As they walked, Rory was investigating his packet of World Cup bubblegum. He had unwrapped the gum, popped it in his mouth, and was now admiring the sticker that had come with it. It showed a dark-haired man in a yellow goalkeeper's shirt. The badge over his heart bore the three lions of England.

Back home in his own era, Rory was a keen collector of Match Attax footballer gamecards. He knew they were *really* meant for kids. But Amy had once bought him a pack as a joke, and that was it – he caught the collecting bug. He now owned an impressive set of twenty-first century Premier League stars. The chance to get his hands on an original "Bazooka" player sticker from the sixty-six World Cup had been too good to miss.

He examined the sticker happily, then looked up at Amy.

'Who did you get?'

'The lovely Norbert "Nobby" Stiles,' replied Amy, holding up her sticker to show him. 'Has a one-in-a-million smile, doesn't he?'

The sticker showed a cheery-looking player, in a white England shirt, who was missing most of his front teeth.

Rory laughed. 'He might need a little dental work, but he's a fantastic player,' he told Amy. 'Toughest tackler we have. Or had, I mean. How about you, Doctor?'

'Hmm? What's that?' As he loped along, the Doctor was browsing the newspaper he had just bought. He looked up distractedly.

Rory waved his sticker. 'Which player did you get?'

'Ah! Right!' said the Doctor. He rolled up his newspaper and slipped it into the left-hand pocket of his tweed jacket. Then he delved in his other jacket pocket for his own penny gum. He unwrapped it, examined the enclosed sticker, and pulled a face.

'Some chap called "Geoff Hurst". Likely-looking fellow. Anyone know if he's any good?'

Rory looked at the Doctor as though he had just asked if the South Pole was at all chilly.

'Not bad, yeah,' he said enviously. 'Just the only player ever to get a hat-trick in a World Cup Final, that's all!'

'*Really*?' said the Doctor. 'A hat-trick, eh? In the final? Excellent!' He regarded the sticker cheerfully for a few seconds, then looked enquiringly at Rory once more. 'And what exactly is a "hat-trick" again?'

Rory was about to reply when he noticed the twinkle in the Doctor's eye. He was having him on.

The Doctor grinned. 'I might not have your encyclopedic knowledge of football trivia, Rory, but I do know a *bit* about the beautiful game,' he said. 'Even played a match or two myself, would you believe? I remember one in particular, when I was standing in for my flatmate –'

'Nah-hah!' interrupted Amy, shaking her head. 'Hold it right there, boys! *No* footballing stories allowed,' she said firmly. 'None. Of any kind. It's bad enough that I let Rory talk me into this trip. I'm about to spend ninety minutes watching a bunch of men, in frankly *very* unflattering shorts, running about after a pig's bladder. I *really* don't need to put up with any macho sports chat from you two on top of that.'

'It'll be a hundred and twenty minutes, actually,' muttered Rory timidly. 'It goes to extra time.'

Amy let out a weary groan.

'Though I think they'll have *slightly* more advanced equipment than you give them credit for, Pond,' added the Doctor. 'Pig's bladder balls were more your nineteenth century. Anyway, I thought you quite liked football?'

'I quite like *footballers*,' Amy corrected him. 'Young, handsome, super-fit, twenty-first century ones. Not middle-aged ones with comb-over hairstyles.' She looked at her picture-card again. 'I mean, Nobby here isn't exactly David Beckham, is he?'

Rory gave her a despairing look.

'It's how you *play* that matters, Amy, not what you look like.'

'Not if you want to win the coveted "Pond Man of the Match" award, it isn't!' replied Amy.

Rory looked a little hurt. Amy looped her arm through his.

'Don't fret, petal!' she said, grinning. 'I'm not really the WAG type. Much happier with a nice ordinary fella than some fat-head with a Ferrari and too much hair gel.'

Rory's expression brightened.

'Although they do *pay* footballers rather better…' Amy teased.

'Not around now, they don't,' replied Rory. 'Players weren't nearly as spoilt, back in the day – even when they got picked for their country. I saw an interview with one of our sixty-six squad once. He said they had to bring their own *towels* to the final!'

'And of course whatever pay they do get will be in old money,' added the Doctor. 'Which is *utterly* baffling.'

Rory smiled at the Doctor. 'I noticed you had a tough time paying that newspaper guy.'

The Doctor looked worried.

'Do you think I gave him enough? I'd hate to have swindled him. Seemed very nice. But he said "sixpence", then asked for a "tanner". Hadn't a *clue* what I was supposed to hand over!'

Amy smirked.

'What are you saying, Doctor? That your big old Time Lord brain can keep the TARDIS ticking over, but can't cope with pounds, shillings and pence?'

The Doctor blew out his cheeks.

'Absolutely! Give me a time-space dimensional

algorithm any day of the week! All this "half-a-sovereign-three-shillings-and-sixpence" business is *terribly* confusing! So many different coins! "Guineas" and "farthings" and "threepenny bits". Last time I was here, someone asked me for "two bob" for something. *Bob*? Does that sound like money to you? It sounds like something you're supposed to *do*, or someone you know.'

He shook his head despairingly.

'Still, it could be worse, I suppose. On Mafooz Minor they use different sized pellets of swamp-vole dung as currency. That's complicated *and* smelly.'

At that moment, a group of young fans jogged past them, clattering their wooden supporters' rattles enthusiastically.

'Those things make a fair old racket, don't they?' said Amy.

Rory's expression became rather glum again.

'I could have topped that, easily,' he said sulkily. 'If it wasn't for a certain person not far away…'

He cast an accusing look at Amy.

'Oh, not *this* again?' Amy groaned. 'It was just a plastic trumpet, Rory. It's gone. Get over it!'

'It wasn't *just* anything,' grumbled Rory. 'It was a proper 2010 World Cup vuvuzela. One of the lads brought it back from South Africa. I was going to be the only person in the crowd with one.'

'Precisely!' Amy snapped back. 'Showing yet again how you spectacularly fail to grasp even the basics of time travel, you clot. Rule Number One – try *not* to stand out.'

'She has a point, Rory,' agreed the Doctor. 'That zulu-wailer wotsit of yours would have looked very out of place. Or time, rather. As Pond says, it's generally a good idea to avoid drawing attention to ourselves.'

Rory gave a snort. 'Oh, right. Of course. Like *you* normally do, you mean?'

The Doctor chose to ignore this.

'On top of which,' he continued, 'it was proving very hard to concentrate on locking the TARDIS onto this precise dateline with you making a sound like a flatulent Zarusian Blubberhog.'

'She still didn't have to snap it in half,' said Rory sulkily.

'Oh, I *so* did!' contradicted Amy. 'It was either that or your neck. The noise was driving me insane!'

'I was practising,' protested Rory. 'They're really hard to blow.'

'You were doing my head in,' Amy corrected him. '*That's* what you were doing.'

'Now, now, children,' smiled the Doctor, 'let's not squabble! After all, Rory, this was your dream destination, remember? And we're here, aren't we? Bang on target. Right place, right time. You're about to get your wish of watching England win the World Cup. I'd have thought you'd be chuffed to bits – toy trumpet or no trumpet.'

'It *wasn't* a toy trumpet!' protested Rory. 'It was a proper vuvu–'

'And unless I'm much mistaken,' continued the Doctor, 'those are the twin towers of the Empire Stadium just up ahead!'

The domed tops of two white towers had just come into view over the heads of the people in front of them. Moments later, the trio got their first proper look at the impressive frontage of the famous stadium.

Rory's sulky mood evaporated in an instant. His vuvuzela was forgotten. The Doctor was right. This trip *was* a dream come true.

'Wow.' Rory came to a standstill. He stood and gawped, happily drinking in the scene. 'Wembley. Real, proper, old-style Wembley.'

His face broke into a massive grin.

'*Wicked!*'

CHAPTER 3

THE MAN FROM FOOFA

The Empire Stadium at Wembley opened to the public in 1923. It hosted a wide range of sporting extravaganzas. Every season's FA Cup Final took place on the Wembley pitch; the World Speedway Championships were decided here; and, in 1948, the stadium was the main venue for the London Olympic Games.

Rory, looking up at the famous Twin Towers, knew that the impressive list of Wembley events would run on into the stadium's future, too. In thirty years time, the final of Euro '96 would be decided at Wembley. And perhaps the most famous rock concert in history, Live Aid, would take place here in 1985, just before he was born.

Right now, though, it was staging the event that would secure its place forever in football folklore. The grand old stadium would be demolished in 2003, to make way for a bigger, bolder Wembley. But thanks to July 30, 1966, it would never be forgotten.

The forecourt was bustling with excited fans, and full of the cries of opportunistic salesmen. Rory noticed a stand selling England rosettes – and also ones in the colours of the top teams of the elite First Division. He was fascinated to see Leeds United and Leicester City among the big name clubs.

Another yelling vendor moved through the crowd not far off.

'Getcha match programmes 'ere! Only two 'n six!'

The Doctor frowned.

'Two *what* and six *what*, though?' he mumbled to himself. 'Or are we supposed to add the two and six together? Eight pounds, perhaps?' He turned to Rory and Amy. 'Is that a lot for a programme? Or not enough?'

The Doctor dug in his trouser pocket, and pulled out a handful of coins. He displayed them on the flat of his palm.

'We should be able to pay for one out of that little lot, don't you think?' The Doctor peered at the assortment of bronze, copper, silver and gold coins. 'Ooo – hang on!' He plucked a thin, blue-tinged disc from the pile. '*That's* a 200,000 Drooble Piece. Only worth anything if you're on Tartac Beta. Barely get you a cup of tea there.'

He thrust the remaining coins towards Rory.

'"Two and six" the man said. If I were you, I'd try two of one sort and six of another. The little twelve-sided ones are rather nice.'

Rory took the money with a wry look.

'Thanks. That's a big help.'

He hurried away to accost the programme seller. It wasn't long before he rejoined them, proudly waving a light-blue match programme.

'Remind me to take this home with us,' Rory told Amy. 'They sell for a *fortune* on Ebay.'

'I reckon our tickets would fetch a fair bit, too,'

agreed Amy.

'Ah. Tickets. Yes.' The Doctor frowned again. 'Now how much do you think *they'll* cost? A lot of bobs?'

Rory looked aghast. 'We don't have tickets already? But there'll be none left! Not for a game like *this*!'

'Good point,' said the Doctor calmly. 'Simpler to do without, anyway.'

'But they'll not let us through the barriers!' said Rory.

The Doctor looked over at the main spectator entrance, through which the fans were steadily flowing.

'Then we'll not go in through the barriers.'

He quickly cast his gaze across the rest of the stadium building.

'We'll go in... *there*!' He pointed to a small grey door in the stadium wall, some distance from the main ticket barriers. A uniformed security guard stood beside it.

'You sure?' said Rory. 'What about the guard? He's hardly going to let us just stroll past. I reckon that entrance is for staff only, or something. Doesn't look like we're supposed to use it.'

'Which is exactly why we're going to,' said the Doctor brightly. 'All the best doors are meant for other people. As for getting past the guard, you forget, Rory – we have something *much* better than tickets.' He delved in the inside pocket of his jacket, then held up a small, blank notepad.

'One access-all-areas stadium pass...'

The security guard took a good long look at the Doctor, then his psychic paper, then the Doctor again.

'You'll have to excuse me, Mr...' – the guard glanced back at the paper – '...Lineker. I'm afraid I've not heard of this "Fair Organisation Of Football Agency" before. What exactly is it you do, sir?'

'Not heard of FOOFA?' The Doctor looked surprised. 'Why, my good man, we're one of the most important regulatory bodies in international sport! As the name suggests, it's our job to make sure that all major soccer competitions are organised in a fair, unbiased way.'

He gestured to Rory, beside him.

'Herr Willhelms here, is from the West German Football Association. I have invited him to visit the team changing rooms to approve the facilities provided for the German squad. To assure him that there is no evidence of favouritism. Cheap, shiny toilet tissue in one team's changing rooms, luxury four-ply in the other – that sort of thing.'

The guard raised his eyebrows.

'And the young lady?' he asked.

'I'm an interpreter,' Amy told the guard curtly. 'Herr Willhelms doesn't speak any English.'

The guard checked the Doctor's credentials again.

'Very well, sir,' he said, with a nod. 'Your pass-card clearly states that you are authorised to visit all areas of the stadium.' He spoke to Amy. 'Please tell the foreign gentleman that I trust he'll find everything above board. We English are very proud of our reputation for fair play.'

Amy turned to Rory. 'Eins zwei drei vier fünf!'

she barked at him, in her best German accent. 'Sechs sieben acht neun zehn!'

Rory nodded first to her, then to the security guard, as though acknowledging his good wishes.

The guard unlocked the grey door, held it open for the FOOFA visitors to pass through, then closed it behind them.

They found themselves in a narrow corridor. Its walls were hung with black and white photographs of famous Wembley winners.

The Doctor nudged Amy with one patched elbow, grinning.

'Good job our guard friend didn't know any German himself, eh, Pond?' he whispered. 'He might have wondered why you were reciting the numbers one to ten!'

'It's the only German I can remember!' Amy hissed back. 'I only did one term of it at school.'

Rory was already engrossed in looking at the old team photographs. But the Doctor bundled him on his way along the corridor.

'Come on! Let's take a look around! We still

have a little while before the match is due to start – plenty of time to find a good spot in the stands. But I bet you'd like a peek at some of the bits that are usually off limits, eh, Rory?'

He strode ahead to where the corridor met another, and turned left. Rory and Amy hurried along behind him. They hadn't gone far when the passageway's right wall became glass. There was a door labelled "Press Room 1". The Doctor stopped and peered through the transparent partition. He turned and smiled at Rory.

'There you go, young man – how about that for starters!'

Rory and Amy, intrigued, peered through the window. The Press Room appeared to have been commandeered for other purposes. Its furniture had been completely rearranged. Chairs were stacked neatly against the walls. In the centre of the cleared floor was a single square table.

The only people in the room were four uniformed police officers. They were stationed at the table's corners, looking outwards. At the centre of the table stood a glass case. Something golden sparkled within it.

'Wow!' hissed Rory. 'That's the cup! The *actual* World Cup!'

'Are you sure?' said Amy. 'It doesn't look much like the pictures *I've* seen. I thought it was a globe? Like a little world, with a bunch of guys holding it up?'

'You're thinking of the *current* trophy,' said Rory. 'This one's the original one. The Jules Rimet Cup. It was replaced with the one you're talking about after Brazil won it for the third time and got to keep it. In 1970.'

Amy looked at him and shook her head.

'Sometimes it frightens me how much of your brain is occupied with footy facts, Williams. You'll never get a girlfriend, you know.'

Rory grinned.

'It's named after the French FIFA president who had the idea for the World Cup in the first place,' he went on. He was enjoying the chance to show off his knowledge. 'It's made out of solid gold, on a lapis lazuli base. It's meant to be Nike, the Greek goddess of victory. You can see her wings, look.'

Amy looked back at the trophy – and at the four burly policeman standing guard over it.

'They're not taking any chances with it, are they?' she said.

'You can't blame them,' said Rory. 'It's been stolen once already. Just a few months back. They put it on display at this fancy stamp exhibition, and someone walked off with it. They never found the thief, but the trophy turned up again a week later. A dog called Pickles sniffed it out, in the bottom of a hedge, when he was out for his morning walk.'

'Clever pooch!' said Amy.

'It gets stolen again later on, too. In 1983, from a bullet-proof glass display cabinet in Brazil. That time, they never get it back.'

One of the police guards was now looking directly across towards them. His expression suggested that he found three faces pressed up against the window rather suspicious.

'Shall we move along?' urged the Doctor.

They hastily drew away from the Press Room window, and set off along the corridor once more. They passed several other side-rooms, but the Doctor strolled purposefully ahead.

'I for one want to see the players' area,' he told them. 'That's right over at the east end.'

As they passed another side-door, Rory came to a halt. There was a sign on it saying "GENTLEMEN". A smaller one underneath read "Officials only".

'Er… guys…' said Rory a little awkwardly. 'If the match is going to last two hours, I could do with popping in here beforehand.'

'Go on then,' said Amy. 'We'll wait.'

'I might be a couple of minutes,' said Rory. 'It's a Gary Neville.'

Amy gave him a blank look.

'Number two,' Rory explained, with a smirk, before ducking through the changing room door.

'Ew!' Amy grimaced. 'Like I needed to know *that*!'

The Doctor raised his eyebrows. 'Do you think there's anything he *can't* put a soccer spin on?'

A few seconds later, they were both surprised to see Rory reappear.

'That was quick!' said Amy.

Rory didn't reply for a moment. His cheery expression had vanished. He looked like he had just had a nasty shock.

'There's something in the toilet,' he told them gravely.

Amy pulled another face.

'Again, *way* more information than we need, Rory!'

'No, not like that!' said Rory. 'In one of the cubicles.'

He looked from Amy to the Doctor, stony-faced.

'It's a body.'

CHAPTER 4

DEAD LUCKY

Inside, the changing room was much like any other. There was a slatted wooden bench running along one wall, with hooks mounted above it; a large sink with a mirror over it; a row of ceramic urinals; and two toilet cubicles. But there was one unusual detail. In the gap beneath the closed door of the left-hand cubicle, the soles of a pair of shoes were just visible.

'It's a bloke,' said Rory in a half-whisper. 'You can tell from his footwear.'

'Genius, Sherlock.' Amy said. 'Although the fact that he's in the *gents* is a *bit* of a clue, too, don't you think?'

The Doctor immediately strode to the closed

cubicle and knocked on its door.

'Hello! Can you hear me? This is the Doctor!'

There was no answer.

'I already tried that,' Rory told the Doctor. 'I even reached under and waggled one of his feet a bit. Nothing.'

'Do you think he's dead?' asked Amy.

'Hard to say without a closer look,' replied the Doctor. 'Could just be deeply unconscious. We need to get this door open.'

Amy fully expected him to produce his sonic screwdriver. But the Doctor just stared at the cubicle door.

'A bog lock shouldn't give your sonic much trouble, should it?' suggested Amy after a few moments.

The Doctor shook his head.

'The lock isn't the problem, Pond. The door opens inwards. Whoever's in there is squashed up against the other side. If they are alive, they won't thank us for squeezing them half to death trying to get the door open.'

'So we need to force it *outwards*, somehow?' said Rory.

'Exactly. Which means using something as a lever… Ah-ha!'

The Doctor suddenly pulled his rolled-up newspaper from his jacket pocket. He took out his sonic screwdriver with the other hand. After a little twiddling of the controls, he touched its glowing tip to the end of the newspaper.

'If I can realign the carbon molecules into a lattice…' he muttered, '…it should increase the rigidity to a high enough degree…' He deactivated the sonic screwdriver and, without warning, gave the toilet door a firm whack with one end of the rolled-up newspaper. It made a loud metallic clang.

'Excellent! Total petrification. Good as an iron bar,' said the Doctor. He quickly set to work on the cubicle door, using the now-rigid newspaper like a crowbar. It didn't take him long to prise the door off its hinges. He and Rory lifted it clear.

The man inside the cubicle was lying on his left side, with his head against the toilet pedestal. He was curled up, his knees drawn up into his chest, his face covered by his raised forearms. He was dressed like many of the male supporters they had seen so far, in a smart suit, white shirt and tie.

Amy helped the Doctor carefully drag the stranger out onto the changing room floor, where there was room to examine him. As Rory checked for signs of breathing, or a pulse, the Doctor scanned his sonic across the man's body. His expression remained grave.

'He *is* dead, right?' said Amy.

Rory nodded grimly. ''Fraid so.'

'Has been for about an hour,' confirmed the Doctor.

'He's not very old, is he?' said Amy sadly. The man looked to be in his mid-twenties. 'What happened, do you think?'

The Doctor was now carrying out a more thorough scan of the man's chest.

'Sudden death in humans is quite often due to a myocardial infarction…'

Amy frowned. 'My-old-cardy'll *what*?'

'A heart attack,' explained Rory.

'Ooo! Get you!' cooed Amy, impressed.

'What?' said Rory. 'I am a nurse, Amy!'

'...but there's no indication of heart failure in this chap's case,' continued the Doctor. 'In fact, he's a picture of health, inside and out. Other than being dead.'

'You think he died from something other than natural causes?' said Amy.

'Possibly. But there's no evidence of violence,' replied the Doctor. 'No swelling from a blow, bleeding from a wound. No trace of toxins, either.'

'Perhaps he had some sort of medical condition,' suggested Rory. He pulled back the man's right jacket sleeve to look at his wrist. 'Did they have medi-alert bracelets in the sixties?'

'Dunno,' said Amy. 'You could check his pockets, too.'

Rory quickly frisked the dead man. He slipped a wallet from an inside jacket pocket, and tossed it to Amy.

'See what you can find out from that.'

Amy began eagerly rifling through the wallet's contents. There was a twinkle in her eye.

'This is just like one of those Amercian TV cop dramas, isn't it?' she said, with a clear note of excitement. 'An unknown corpse. You two, the guys who do all that forensic-y pathology stuff. Me, the glamorous, super-brainy female detective trying to piece together the victim's identity…' Her face lit up. 'I'm in Crime Scene Investigation! CSI Wembley!'

Both Rory and the Doctor glanced up from examining the body. Their disapproving looks wiped the smile off Amy's face. She adopted an expression of exaggerated seriousness.

'Sorry. Obviously I'm not *enjoying* this. Not when someone has died. That would be wrong. Clearly.'

'Found anything yet to suggest *which* someone, Detective Inspector Pond?' the Doctor asked.

Amy turned her attention back to the wallet's contents.

'Not really,' she said. 'There's not much here.

Nothing with an ID, anyway. No credit cards. But I guess people didn't carry plastic in 1966, did they? There's just a couple of big old one pound notes. Cute.'

She tried another compartment in the back of the wallet.

'Hang on. There's this, too.'

She pulled out a small slip of paper, and took a closer look at it.

'It's some sort of receipt, I think. Dated yesterday. From William Hill. That's one of those betting shops, isn't it?'

'Let's have a look,' said Rory. Amy passed him the slip of paper.

'Yeah, it's a betting chit,' said Rory. 'He must have put some money on a horse. Someone's written on the back of it. "Hot to Trot. 200 to 1. Ten pounds, to win."'

Amy frowned. 'Hot to Trot,' she repeated. 'I've heard that somewhere before. I'm *sure* I have...'

She clicked her fingers.

'Got it! It was when we stopped at that

newspaper stand on the way here. There was a sports bulletin playing on that guy's radio. The lead story was about this no-hoper horse that had won a big race. Hot to Trot. That was definitely what it was called.'

Rory passed the betting chit back to her.

'Well, if you're right, this chap just won a small fortune. At those odds, he'd have picked up two grand in winnings. And round about now, two thousand pounds is a *lot* of money. We're talking enough to buy a house.'

Amy looked at the dead man pityingly.

'What a rubbish time to snuff it. Like winning the lottery, then keeling over before you can spend it.'

'Do you think maybe he works here?' asked Rory.

'What makes you say that?'

'Well otherwise, how come he's allowed in here? "Officials only" it said on the door.'

Rory suddenly pulled something from the man's trouser pocket. It was a piece of printed card, about ten centimetres square, in a leather sleeve. Rory looked it over.

'I think I just found my answer. Listen to this.' He read out the text from the card. '"VIP World Cup Final Stadium Pass. Issued to the winner of the Daily Express World Cup Spot-the-Ball Challenge".'

'Blimey,' said Amy. 'So this guy had just won a fortune on the horses *and* a nationwide newspaper competition. He was having a seriously lucky day, wasn't he?'

'Up until the moment of his sudden, lonely death, you mean?' said Rory.

'Point taken.'

The Doctor finished examining the body. He stood up, frowning.

'I can't find any obvious cause of death. Maybe there's a clue in *where* we found him.' He moved into the doorless cubicle, and began looking around inside it. 'Why would he have locked himself in here, do you think?'

Rory gave the Doctor an amused look.

'Er, you mean *apart* from the obvious reason?'

'Yes, Rory, I do.' The Doctor lifted one side of the toilet cistern cover. He buzzed his sonic over the water inside for a second or two. He replaced the cistern cover, then lifted the lid of the toilet itself and peered into the bowl. 'There's no evidence of him having used the loo.'

Amy smirked at Rory. 'Not like when *you've* been, then.'

Rory ignored her. 'How can you tell?' he asked the Doctor. 'He'd have flushed it, wouldn't he?'

'The water in the cistern is at room temperature,' explained the Doctor. 'Which means it's been in there long enough to equalise with its surroundings. This toilet hasn't been flushed for several hours.'

'I'm losing that cool TV cop show vibe now,' muttered Amy. 'They tend not to major on loo flushing.'

'Maybe he was just *about* to go,' said Rory.

'Boys!' Amy looked despairing. 'Enough already with the detailed toilet analysis! Can't we dust for DNA or something?'

'Or *maybe*,' the Doctor pressed on, ignoring her, 'maybe he wasn't in there to use the toilet at all. Look how he's lying. Back curved, knees up, hands covering his face. The foetal position. The posture of an unborn child. Humans instinctively revert to it when they feel defenceless. And look at his eyes. They're screwed tight shut.'

Amy looked at the Doctor.

'You're saying he came in here, locked himself in, and curled up in a ball – because he was *frightened*?'

'Exactly, Pond.'

'Frightened of what?' said Rory.

'No idea,' said the Doctor. 'But I intend to find out.' He knelt beside the man's body again. 'I *must* have missed something. I'll take another set of bio-readings. You two check if he has anything else on him.'

Rory obediently began a repeat search of the man's trouser pockets. Amy rooted around in his jacket to see if Rory had overlooked anything there.

After a few seconds of silence, the Doctor suddenly let out a triumphant cry.

'Ah-hah! Now *that* makes things a *lot* more interesting!' He was running the tip of his sonic slowly across the man's forehead.

'What is it, Doctor?' asked Amy.

'I can't find any evidence of endorphins anywhere in his system. Not even the faintest of traces. There shou–'

But before the Doctor could explain further, something happened that brought their investigation to an abrupt halt.

The changing room door swung open and a tall, middle-aged man strode through. He was smartly dressed, and carrying a large green kitbag. He had silver hair, but very dark, thick eyebrows, and an impressive, almost black moustache.

The man stopped dead in his tracks, his shock obvious in his face. Amy, Rory and the Doctor could hardly have looked more suspicious. A group of strangers, in a restricted area, going through the pockets of a corpse.

The man's wide-eyed gaze flitted to the forced cubicle door propped against the wall behind them, then back to the trio.

Amy smiled sweetly. This was going to take a *lot* of explaining.

CHAPTER 5

THE RUSSIAN LINESMAN

The man with the moustache let his kitbag drop to the floor. He stepped forward towards the three friends, scowling fiercely. He growled something accusingly at them, in a language that neither Rory nor Amy could understand.

The Doctor was on his feet in a flash. He hurried to greet the newcomer.

'Hello there!' he said, beaming amiably. 'The name's Lineker! We're here from FOOFA. Having a spot of bother, as you can see!'

The man growled something else incomprehensible. It sounded equally hostile.

'Yes, I can imagine this must look *very* bad from where you're standing!' said the Doctor, still smiling. 'What dark thoughts must be running through that mind of yours, eh?'

As he said this, he gave the scowling stranger a harmless tap on the forehead with his rolled newspaper, still clutched in his left hand.

At least, it was *meant* to be harmless. What the Doctor had forgotten, for an absent-minded moment, was that the paper was now as hard as iron.

The blow sent the moustached man staggering backwards. His heels hit his discarded kitbag, and he toppled helplessly over it. As he fell, the back of his head hit one corner of the tiled wall. He slumped to the floor, and lay still.

'Oh, great!' cried Amy. She and Rory jumped up and came to join the mortified Doctor. He was already bent over his unintended victim, hastily checking his vital signs.

'Nice going, Doctor!' said Amy. 'Nothing keeps a murder mystery alive like another dead body. Forget CSI – this is getting more like an Agatha Christie plot. Or Cluedo. "It was the

Doctor, in the changing room, with the iron newspaper."'

'I haven't *killed* him, Amy!' said the Doctor defensively. 'He's just unconscious.' He continued to administer first aid, the sonic screwdriver buzzing once more.

Rory, meanwhile, was staring at the newcomer's face.

'That's weird,' he muttered. 'I've seen this bloke before. I'm certain I have. I recognise that tash...'

He bent down to unzip the stranger's kitbag, and began rummaging inside. The first thing he pulled out was a small orange flag on a short wooden stem. He replaced this, and lifted out an item of clothing. It was a black, long-sleeved sports shirt with white cuffs and collars. Rory examined the name label stitched inside the shirt's collar.

The colour was rapidly draining from Rory's face.

'Oh, no,' he mumbled. 'No, no, no...'

'What's the matter?' Amy looked at the black shirt Rory was staring at with such obvious dismay.

'That's a referee's kit, isn't it?'

'Not a referee's,' replied Rory miserably. 'This bloke is a match official, all right. But not the ref. He's a linesman. Tofik Bakhramov. The *Russian* linesman…'

'Azerbaijani,' said the Doctor, without looking up.

'Bless you,' said Amy.

'No. This man. He's from Azerbaijan, not Russia,' explained the Doctor. 'In Eastern Europe. It's obvious from his accent.'

'Yeah. Right. Obvious,' said Amy. 'If you're some sort of anorak-y accent spotter.'

'The term is "linguist", Pond.'

'OK, OK,' said Rory impatiently. 'So maybe he's from Azerbaijan, not Russia. Whatever. All I know is he's famous as the Russian Linesman.'

'Famous?' Amy looked at Rory. 'Famous how?'

'I can't believe you don't know! I thought *everyone* English knew about th–'

Rory noticed the fiery glint behind Amy's narrowing eyes just in time. Amy was Scottish, *not*

English. And it didn't pay to forget it.

'He's famous for helping England beat Germany in the sixty-six final,' Rory stated simply.

'What – you mean he cheated? The match was fixed?'

'No, nothing as dodgy as that. He made a really tough call in England's favour. The whole match was finely balanced – two goals a piece after ninety minutes. Then Hurst scored another in extra time to put England 3-2 up. Only it wasn't a *definite* goal. Hurst's shot hit the crossbar and rebounded down onto the goal line. It only counted because the Russian linesman – Bakhramov, here – told the referee that the ball had crossed the line.'

'Shame they didn't have goal line technology,' observed Amy.

Rory stared at her. He was clearly stunned to hear her offer such an informed opinion.

'What?' said Amy. 'I read about it somewhere. About some dodgy decision in the last World Cup. When Frank Lampard scored, but the ref said the ball hadn't crossed the line. And about how it wouldn't have happened if they'd had "goal line technology". Whatever that is.'

Rory stuffed the linesman's shirt back into the kitbag.

'It still makes me sick just thinking about that Lampard no-goal,' he said bitterly. 'That was against Germany, too. It would have made it 2-2. Instead, we lost 4-1.' He shook his head sadly. 'A lot of England fans think that decision sealed the match.'

Rory pointed at the unconscious stranger. The Doctor was still bent over him, busy with his sonic screwdriver.

'This bloke made a crucial decision just like that, back in sixty-six. Only then, it was in the final, and it went England's way. He plays a vital part in England's victory. And the Doctor has just knocked his lights out!'

At that moment, the Doctor stood up, looking greatly relieved.

'There, all done!' He noticed Rory's glum expression. 'Don't worry, Rory! He'll make a full recovery. I've triggered the blood vessels around the point of impact to dilate, so there's no danger of compression. And I've made sure he'll stay under for a little while. Won't wake for at least a couple of hours, I shouldn't think. That'll give the accelerated tissue repair I've set in motion more than enough time to take effect. When he comes round, he'll be right as rain.'

If anything, Rory looked even *more* miserable.

'You're totally missing the point, Doctor! Didn't you hear what I've been saying? England *need* Bakhramov at the match! He's going to miss it now, isn't he? When he doesn't turn up, he'll be replaced by someone else – someone who might *not* allow England's third goal. Which means the result could go a different way. We might not win.'

He glared at the Doctor accusingly.

'There's a good chance you've just single-handedly lost us the World Cup!'

CHAPTER 6
A CHANGED MAN

Rory looked very disappointed that his dramatic announcement hadn't caused more of a stir. He clearly felt he had just dropped a bombshell. The Doctor and Amy were supposed to be horror-struck. As it was, neither of them looked very bothered.

'Don't get your knickers in a twist, Rory,' said Amy. 'England'll probably still be okay. Even without this Bak-wotsit bloke. They're supposed to win 4-2, aren't they? So they can spare one goal anyway, can't they?'

'No!' protested Rory. 'That's not how football works! A big decision can tip a match one way or the other. If their third goal isn't allowed, the lads might lose heart. They'd be going into the last period of extra time all square. The result could go either way!'

'A replacement linesman might still award the goal, Rory,' pointed out the Doctor.

'He *might*, yeah!' Rory turned to Amy. 'And England could *probably* still win. But that's not good enough, is it? We're talking about *the only time we've ever won the World Cup*! And we may have messed that up!'

The Doctor still showed no sign of sharing Rory's panic. But his expression did become more grave. He strode over to stand beside the body they had discovered in the toilet cubicle.

'For the moment, Rory, I'm more worried about what happened to this lucky chap.'

'You mean "*un*lucky",' Amy corrected him.

The Doctor shook his head.

'No, Pond. It's his recent *good* luck that interests me. I have an idea that it holds the key to his death. And if I'm right, there may be more important things at stake than the World Cup.'

Amy frowned. 'What do you m–'

'*More important than England winning the World Cup?*' spluttered Rory. He was looking at the Doctor as if he had completely lost the plot. 'Like *what*?'

But if the Doctor had been about to explain his theory, he must have thought better of it.

'Never mind. You're probably right, Rory. We ought to do something about this Bakhramov chap. If he's missing from the match, it *is* possible it could turn out differently. And the sixty-six World Cup Final isn't a piece of history I particularly want the responsibility for rewriting. Even accidentally.'

He stared at Bakhramov's body in silence for a few seconds, lost in thought. Then he clicked his fingers, and became his usual animated self.

'Okay, Rory. Panic not. I have a plan. I have right *here*...' He delved into the left-hand pocket of his tweed jacket, rooted about for a few moments, then pulled a face. 'Or perhaps here...' He tried the other pocket, and with a look of relief pulled out something small, metallic and disc-shaped, with a slim strap attached. 'Voilà! The solution to our dilemma!'

'A watch?' said Rory. 'I've already got a watch. How is a watch going to help?'

'Not a watch. A *shimmer*,' announced the Doctor. 'A piece of highly advanced morphing technology manufactured by the master craftsmen of the Vinvocci. You know the Vinvocci? Green-skinned humanoids. Rather a lot of alarmingly spiky bits. Otherwise delightful.'

'It's a stroke of luck I still have this on me,' continued the Doctor. 'It's been in my pocket since our visit to the *Neutrino Casino*. Back on Vegas IV, remember?'

'You bet I do!' said Amy. 'I won't forget that poker game in a hurry. Who'd have guessed aliens play such a mean game of cards? Only time I've played against someone with *three* poker faces. I was cleaning up, too, till that big hairy goon ate my betting chips.'

'I did warn you, Pond. Never play cards with a Moslovian. Anyway, where was I? Ah, yes. Vegas.

Do you recall the karaoke competition they were running in the casino bar?'

'Sure,' said Amy. 'All those awful Elvis Presley impersonators, competing to be "Cosmic King". It's hard to forget. It was like The X Factor with aliens. Extra-terrestrial Factor.' She snorted. 'Although there was *one* of them who was pretty good. Came third, I think.'

The Doctor looked at her, raised his eyebrows, and gave an impish grin.

'No?!' Amy's brown eyes widened with surprise. '*You*? Honest?'

'Uh-huh-huh!' replied the Doctor, Elvis-style.

'I wondered where you'd slunk off to!' said Amy, grinning. 'But that third-place guy didn't look anything *like* you! He was a dead ringer for Presley!'

'I was indeed,' agreed the Doctor. 'And all thanks to this little beauty.' He held up the shimmer. 'As I said, it's a morphing device. Changes what you look like – from the neck up, at least. It masks the wearer's actual physical appearance and projects a remarkably convincing fake one in its place.'

He took hold of Rory's left arm and began hastily fastening the shimmer around it, just above his normal wristwatch.

'A word of advice though, Rory.' The Doctor snapped closed the shimmer's magna-strap. 'Leave it switched off until you need it. The masking field can make you feel quite ill once it's running. That's why I had to drop out of the last karaoke round on Vegas. Too queasy to make it through "All Shook Up".' He grinned. 'Ironic, really.'

Rory lifted his wrist, looked at the alien device now strapped to it, then back at the Doctor. He shook his head.

'No. Sorry. I'm not getting it. How will me looking like Elvis help? How does that change the fact you just took out the Russian linesman?'

'Azerbaijani,' said Amy. Rory scowled at her.

'You're not going to look like *Elvis*,' explained the Doctor impatiently. He quickly took out his sonic screwdriver, and crouched down beside the unconscious Bakhramov. He began slowly scanning the sonic's glowing tip back and forth across the linesman's face. 'A Vinvoccian shimmer can be programmed to mimic almost *any* physical appearance.'

He completed his forehead-to-chin scan of Bakhramov's features, and stood up. Turning back to Rory, he took hold of his left wrist again, and gingerly touched the tip of his sonic screwdriver to the flat face of the shimmer. He held it there for a few moments. There was a soft bleep from the shimmer, and a pulse of red light swirled once around its outer rim.

'There!' said the Doctor. 'You're all set! I've overwritten the facial modelling data. Give it a try. Just twist the dial casing to activate it.'

Rory was still looking completely lost. But he did as he was told. He twisted the shimmer's dial.

Amy's eyes widened with astonishment.

'Wow. Now *that* is *properly* spooky,' she said, impressed. She looked from Rory to the unconscious linesman, then back again. 'They're like twins! Even the tash is spot on...'

The Doctor smiled. He clapped Rory on the shoulder.

'So – problem solved!' he said cheerfully. 'One instant replacement Mr Bakhramov. As long as you're wearing the shimmer, and have it turned on, nobody will know you're not the real thing.'

Rory was slowly catching on. He pointed to the unconscious linesman.

'You want *me* to impersonate *him*?'

'It's not what *I* want, Rory. It's what *you* want,' replied the Doctor. 'To save the match, remember. England expects, and all that. And don't look so worried. You'll do splendidly!'

He grabbed Bakhramov's kitbag from the floor and thrust it at Rory.

'All you have to do is get changed into this little lot, and get yourself out on the pitch in time for kick-off.'

'But…'

'Then *you* can personally see to it that that goal line decision goes England's way, yes?'

'But I'm not…'

'Because *you'll* be the one making it. Simple. Can't fail. Well, not unless it does.'

Rory gave up. He silently took the kitbag from the Doctor, turned, and skulked across to the changing bench, shaking his head the whole time.

'As for you and I, Pond...'

The Doctor held out his sonic screwdriver at arm's length. He began moving it in arcs and sweeps, like an instrument of magic. He squinted at its luminous green tip intently for a few seconds.

'...I think *we* should get ourselves over to the South Stand,' he muttered, fully focussed on the sonic's flickers and pulses.

'You're still planning to watch the match, then?' asked Amy.

The Doctor appeared not to hear.

'Actually, make that *under* the South Stand,' he muttered. He finally lowered the sonic screwdriver, and turned to face Amy. 'We may have a little business to conduct there.'

'What kind of "business"?'

'But we probably ought to tidy up a bit first,'

rambled the Doctor, failing once again to answer Amy. 'I should be able to patch up that door...' He looked at the pair of bodies lying on the floor. 'Let's get these two somewhere out of sight to start with. You grab our linesman friend –'

'*Doctor*!' Amy was getting annoyed. 'What *kind* of business?'

The Doctor gave her a cheery look. 'Oh, you know, Pond. Usual sort of thing.'

He reached down to grab the dead man's feet. As he began dragging the corpse towards the door, he looked over his shoulder at Amy.

'Just a deadly alien life-form to hunt down.'

Amy watched the Doctor reverse out through the door. She gave a resigned sigh, bent down to grasp Bakhramov's ankles, and set off after him, dragging the unconscious linesman behind her.

''Course. Deadly alien hunt. Silly me for asking.'

CHAPTER 7

ON THE SPOT

Rory was feeling extremely peculiar. The fact that he had now been wearing the shimmer for some time was undoubtedly one reason his insides felt like he was on a rough ferry crossing. The Doctor had warned him about this unfortunate side-effect of using the Vinvoccian device.

But it wasn't *only* the shimmer that was making Rory feel uncomfortable. The churning in his stomach was as much to do with the situation in which he now found himself.

He was standing in the mouth of the Wembley players' tunnel, about to lead out the teams for the most momentous football match in English history, in front of a crowd of 93,000 screaming fans. Not to mention the largest ever TV audience of over 32 million people. This wasn't the sort of thing that happened to most ordinary lads from Leadworth.

Rory glanced nervously at the other two match officials standing beside him. So far, neither of them seemed to have noticed anything suspicious. Apart from its unfortunate side-effects, the shimmer was working a treat. Now that he was wearing Bakhramov's full black-and-white kit, Rory was the spitting image of the Azerbaijani linesman. Even Bakhramov's friends and family would not have seen through the disguise – unless by noticing that he had inexplicably lost a few centimetres in height.

Rory's biggest worry had been what to do if someone spoke to him. He might *look* like Bakhramov, but he had no clever alien gadget to make him *sound* like him.

So far, however, he'd been lucky. He had only needed to return the occasional nod of acknowledgement, smile, or gesture. In fact, it was becoming clear that none of the officials expected to talk much. Rory vaguely recalled something from a TV programme on the 1966 final about the language barrier between them. He was fairly sure the referee was from Switzerland. And the other linesman was Czech, wasn't he? If the three of them had no common language, he'd hopefully be able to bluff his way through whatever communication was required. The odd shout, hand signal, or bit of flag-waving might just see him through.

Rory looked over his shoulder, back down the sloping concrete shaft of the player's tunnel – and felt his stomach do another cartwheel. The tunnel was crammed with footballing legends. At the head of the line of players on the right-hand side of the tunnel, wearing red shirts, white shorts and red socks, stood the blonde-haired English captain, Bobby Moore. On the opposite side, West German captain and centre-forward Uwe Seeler was in position to lead out his ten team mates. The Germans were wearing their white-and-black first kit.

Rory's eyes darted from player to player. There was Geoff Hurst, right there; Bobby Charlton, the legendary English midfielder; Jackie, his elder brother; Alan Ball, the youngest in the squad, who would win "Man of the Match" in this epic final. And there, in the German line-up, a young Franz Beckenbauer, another of the greatest players of all time, who Rory knew would go on to captain the World Cup-winning team in 1974, *and* coach the German squad that triumphed in the 1990 tournament. These were footballers Rory had admired all his life. He had watched the black-and-white TV footage and glorious Technicolor Pathé films of their historic sixty-six clash many times. And now here they were, metres away, in the flesh.

A nudge from the referee drew Rory's attention. The ref was tapping his stopwatch. It was evidently time for the teams to make their way out onto the pitch. Without further ado, the Swiss official led the way.

Rory took a deep breath, tried to get his insides

to stop churning like a washing machine on spin, and set off after him.

A little over ten minutes later, Rory found himself one of a small group of five men – the three match officials and both team captains – gathered within the centre circle of the Wembley pitch.

The short spell since the teams had emerged from the players' tunnel had not been without a few sticky moments. During the playing of the teams' national anthems, Rory had been so caught up in the moment, he had very nearly joined in with the crowd's rousing rendition of "God Save the Queen". Thankfully, he had come to his senses just in time. A match official from Eastern Europe belting out the English anthem would have looked rather suspicious.

The Royal Box was directly above the stadium's main entrance tunnel. The world champions would climb the famous thirty-nine steps that ran up to it to receive their winner's medals from Her Majesty, Queen Elizabeth. Rory had a good view of the dark-haired queen, in her striking yellow coat and hat. He was struck by how young she looked.

After the anthems, the English and German teams had shaken hands, then jogged out across the pitch's "hallowed turf" to warm up. As the players began kicking about the match-balls they had carried out with them, Rory noted how basic these were. The plain, orangey-brown leather ball looked a lot less flashy than the high-spec ones used in top-level twenty-first century football.

There were many other ways in which the scene around him differed greatly from the world of football with which Rory was familiar. For one thing, many of the spectators were standing. Rory was used to modern all-seater stadiums. Fans from both nations were mixed in together, too. West German flags waved here and there among a sea of Union Jacks. There was no dugout for coaches and substitutes. In fact, there was no substitutes' bench, full stop. Player substitutions weren't allowed in early tournaments, Rory recalled. Only four men sat on the England team bench, at the side of the pitch – the manager and his coaching team, all wearing pale blue tracksuits.

Before Rory had time to take in more than a few period details, he found himself being led by the Swiss referee to the centre of the pitch.

Now, as he stood at the very heart of it all, with kick-off only moments away, Rory continued to marvel at the noise and spectacle. The volume of the crowd had somehow risen even further. The atmosphere was like nothing he had ever experienced.

He watched Moore and Seeler, the team captains, exchange national tokens and shake hands sportingly. Then they stepped back to allow the referee room for the coin toss. Rory, looking on, found it rather bizarre to be the only person in the ground who already knew that Moore would win the toss, and choose to let the Germans take the kick.

As Moore withdrew from the centre-circle, the referee turned to Rory and his fellow linesman and gestured to his watch once more. He was signalling for them to check their timekeeping devices, Rory realised, so as to be sure they were synchronised.

Rory instinctively went to pull up his left sleeve in order to check his watch – then changed his mind. Exposing his shimmer would be a very bad idea. The advanced alien technology of the Vinvocci did not belong in the sixties. Besides, having *two* watches would seem weird enough. Instead, he slipped his hand under the cuff of his sleeve and glanced down, pretending to check.

A moment later, the referee gestured for both linesmen to take up their positions. The Czech official jogged off towards the touchline in front of the South Stand. Rory gratefully hurried away to take up his own assigned position. It would be his job – or, rather, it should have been Bakhramov's – to keep an eye on play within the half of the pitch furthest from the players' tunnel. England would start the match defending his end.

As he crossed the pitch, Rory felt his pulse quickening. His experience as a football official was limited, to say the least – one stint as referee at an informal match after a friend's wedding, between the bride and groom's male relatives. That was it. And *that* game had ended in a brawl. And here he was, at Wembley, trying to pass himself off as a linesman of international standing.

Anxious last-minute thoughts flooded Rory's brain. Even some of the laws of the game were different back in 1966, weren't they? Wasn't the goalkeeper only allowed three strides carrying the ball, or something? And what about passing back to the keeper? The rules about that had changed, too, hadn't they?

Mind racing, Rory reached the touchline. Feeling sicker than ever, he turned to face the field of battle. The players had already taken up their positions. Somewhere beneath his panic and nausea, Rory's mind registered the familiar formations: Germany were playing four up front, with wingers; England had a four-four-two shape, with Nobby Stiles in a slightly deeper, more defensive position than his three fellow midfielders.

The two German centre-forwards were at the spot now. Seeler had the ball at his feet. Rory saw the referee put his whistle to his lips, and heard its shrill blast. He gripped the wooden shaft of his linesman's flag more tightly.

They were off.

CHAPTER 8

THE SOUTH STAND

Amy peered ahead into the gloom, and frowned. She turned to the Doctor, beside her, who was fiddling with his sonic screwdriver.

'So what exactly am I looking out for, Doctor? An itsy-bitsy cute-looking alien, or something a bit more, you know –'

She pulled a monster-style face, clawed at the air with her hands, and stomped her feet.

'Embarrassing?' ventured the Doctor.

Amy scowled.

'I was doing "scary".'

She and the Doctor had now spent ten minutes or more searching the area under the South Stand. They had gained entry through a locked (not for long) maintenance doorway. The Doctor had led the way into the murky forest of dark grey columns that lay beyond – the sturdy metal struts of the grandstand's steel skeleton. He had kept his eyes fixed on the flickering tip of his sonic screwdriver. Amy had followed, ducking under crossbeams now and again, and trying not to stumble on the roughly cast concrete underfoot. With only the sonic screwdriver's glow to light the way, it was fairly slow going. But by now, thought Amy, they *must* be right under the centre of the grandstand.

And so far, there had been no sign of any alien creature.

'Sorry, Pond,' said the Doctor. 'Haven't a clue what it might *look* like, I'm afraid. All we know is that it's some kind of luck-sucker.'

'Excuse me?'

'A luck-sucker. A neural parasite.'

'And again, excuse me?'

The Doctor left off re-calibrating his sonic screwdriver for a moment to give Amy his full attention.

'We know that poor chap back in the gents had been on a remarkable run of good fortune, prior to his death. Yes?'

Amy nodded.

'After the run of luck he'd been having,' continued the Doctor, 'he must have been feeling on top of the world this morning. His blood would have contained unusually high levels of endorphins.'

'Which are?' said Amy. 'In normal-person-speak, please.'

'Bio-chemicals which make you feel euphoric,' explained the Doctor. 'They generate the feel-good rush.'

'Yup, remembering now!' said Amy. 'Eating chocolate makes you release them, right?'

'Indeed. Among other things. The point is, they're linked with the sort of emotional high our friend must have been on. But my bio-scans picked up no trace of any recent endorphin surge. Quite the opposite. From my sonic readings, you would have thought that the poor fellow hadn't felt happy in days.'

'So the guy was a bit of a misery.' Amy gave a shrug. 'Why has that got us hunting aliens?'

'He wasn't a "bit of a misery",' Amy. 'He must have felt delighted – ecstatic, even – when he won that horse racing bet. But something drained every trace of that positive energy from his body.'

'Our mystery alien?'

'Exactly,' said the Doctor. 'I've come across several species that feed on the positive neural energy of others. Neural parasites. They target those experiencing high levels of good fortune and extremes of happiness, and drain the resulting positive energy from them. Some folk call them "Happiness Vampires". Or "Luck-suckers".'

Amy shivered.

'Sounds creepy. Kinda like the Dementors™ in *Harry Potter*™?'

'I suppose. Except *real*,' replied the Doctor. 'Some species only drain off small quantities of neural energy, then move on. The host is left relatively unharmed – just a little low-spirited. But others drain everything they can –'

'And you end up dead in a toilet, right?'

'Not necessarily in a toilet. But dead, yes.'

'So *that's* what we're looking for?' said Amy. 'An alien luck-sucker?'

The Doctor nodded.

'And you're sure it's under here somewhere?'

'Almost certain,' the Doctor held up his sonic screwdriver. Its tip was pulsing regularly. 'I'm picking up clear signs of non-human life-form activity. My sonic screwdriver detected them even back in the changing room.'

'Couldn't they be coming from rats, or something?' suggested Amy. 'Or really big spiders?' She paused. 'On second thoughts, I might prefer a nice alien.'

'No, it's something non-terrestrial. Or I'm a Raxacoricofallapatorian.'

The Doctor slowly scanned the sonic screwdriver to his right. His face lit up as its tip flared brightly.

'There, you see!' the Doctor excitedly thrust the screwdriver towards Amy. 'Look at that, Pond!

If it was all just concrete and steel under here, I wouldn't be getting a bio-thermal reading like *that*, now, would I?'

Amy hadn't the faintest idea which bit of the sonic screwdriver she was supposed to be looking at. 'Absolutely not,' she said solemnly. 'That would be silly.'

'Come on!' The Doctor turned to his right and strode away purposefully. 'This way!'

Amy did her best to keep up, picking her way through the metal maze of girders as fast as she could. She spotted one crossbeam a moment too late.

'Ow!' Amy stopped to nurse her head. She had hit it quite hard. 'Arrrggh!' she growled, rubbing her forehead. 'Whatever our wretched alien is, I wish it had picked a nicer place to hang out!'

The Doctor didn't reply. He had come to an abrupt halt just ahead of her. He had suddenly become very still, and was peering ahead silently into the gloom.

'Doctor?'

The Doctor turned, eyes sparkling. 'You've put

your finger right on it again, Pond!' he whispered excitedly.

Amy looked defensive. 'What?' she hissed back, not sure why they were whispering. 'I didn't touch anything!'

'No, I mean – *look*!' The Doctor bundled her forward, and pointed into the gloom. 'A place to hang out is *exactly* what they were after…'

Up ahead, about twenty metres or so from where she and the Doctor were standing, Amy could make out some pale shapes amid the darkness. As she concentrated her gaze, the Doctor increased the intensity of his sonic screwdriver's glow a little, to cast a bit more light.

Dangling from one of the higher crossbeams of the grandstand's metal framework was a row of twenty or so large, pale grey, sack-like objects. Each of the flabby capsules was nearly three metres long, and had a slight ribbing to its shape, like the body of a maggot. The sacks hung from the girder by thick bands of sticky-looking webbing. They glistened, as though wet.

Midway along the row, Amy saw two sacks

that looked different to the rest. They were ripped from top to bottom, as though they had burst. She could see that they were empty inside, except for the almost luminous silvery ooze that coated their inner walls.

Amy flinched as she saw one of the sacks next to the burst ones twitch. Something inside it had moved.

'Look! There are more over there!' hissed the Doctor. Amy followed his gaze. Away to the left, a second row of grey sacks dangled from another grandstand beam. She could just make out more rows in the murk behind them, too. There must be hundreds.

Amy had no idea what was inside the peculiar grey sacks. Or rather, in the case of the two burst ones, what *had* been inside. But she knew one thing for sure.

They gave her the creeps.

Big time.

CHAPTER 9
NOT QUITE BUTTERFLIES

'What *are* they, Doctor?' hissed Amy.

'Vispic leeches.' The Doctor smacked the heel of one palm against his tall forehead. 'Of *course*! Vispics fit our suspect profile perfectly!' He stared at the row upon row of dangling sacks. 'But I've never seen a brood so large!'

At that moment, a pinpoint of orange light suddenly appeared in the darkness ahead of them.

'And it looks like they're still arriving...' murmured the Doctor.

The dot of light flared and widened, quickly becoming a perfect circle, nearly a metre across. Amy had the distinct impression that the light was shining *through* – as if the circle were a hole in the air, admitting the orange glow from somewhere behind it.

She watched in horror as something pale and wet began to wriggle out of the hole in the air. A bulbous, maggoty body slowly squirmed its way through. It was off-white, with blotches of grey. Its flattened head – if that was what the first end to appear was – was dotted with dark, fibrous patches. It reminded Amy of the exposed surface of a verruca.

As it dragged its tail-end free, the wriggling thing flopped onto the concrete floor with an unpleasant squelch. The luminous hole immediately shrunk back to a pinpoint, then vanished.

Amy watched, transfixed, as the newly appeared creature slowly squirmed itself across the floor to one of the vertical steel columns. It began to wriggle its way up towards a horizontal beam from which several of the pale grey sacks already dangled.

'Is *that* what's inside each of those pouchy-things?' Amy asked the Doctor.

'The cocoons? Yes.'

'Yuck.' Amy watched the creature squirm slowly up the column. 'It doesn't look particularly "deadly", though,' she observed. 'Gross, yeah. But not dangerous.'

The Doctor gave her a dark look. 'Tell that to our friend back in the changing room.'

'But how did one of those things even get near him?' asked Amy. 'They look way too... *sluggy* to corner anyone.'

'They didn't need to corner him,' said the Doctor. 'Vispics can drain neural energy from a host without any physical contact. As long as they can get within a reasonable range, they can feed at will.

'From under here, they'd have been able to latch onto that poor chap we found without any difficulty. Once they'd begun feeding, he would have felt a growing sense of inexplicable unhappiness, fear and ultimately utter terror. It would have driven him to lock himself away, in a desperate attempt to hide – though he would have had no idea what from.'

'Sounds horrible,' said Amy.

'Indeed. And as the Vispics drained away the last of his neural energy, he would simply have lost the will to live.' The Doctor shook his head sadly. 'Dreadful.'

He was silent for a moment or two.

'And don't be fooled into thinking that Vispics are *always* sluggish, Pond. You're looking at their young. Their larval form. They're a species that metamorphose as they mature. Change form entirely. In time, given the right conditions, an adult leech will emerge from each of those cocoons.'

The Doctor peered across at the nearest row of dangling sacks.

'In fact, judging by those burst ones, I'd say some already have.'

Amy was still watching the larva in horrified fascination. It had now squirmed its way out along the horizontal girder. It was busy securing its tail-end to it with a blob of sticky goo it had just secreted.

'So – they're sort of like caterpillars turning into butterflies?'

'A little bit, yes,' said the Doctor. 'If you can imagine a caterpillar that feeds on neural energy rather than cabbage. And instead of a butterfly, a large, ultra-intelligent, ruthless predator. With pincers. And no pretty wings.'

'The grown-ups are that bad, huh?'

'If you're after classic chase-you-and-eat-you scary, Pond, an adult Vispic is about as good as it gets.'

Amy gave him a hard look.

'You say that like you're impressed. Got a real thing for monsters, haven't you? It's like being out and about with one of those loony wildlife presenters who only seek out the deadliest animals. The ones that like prodding snakes or winding up crocodiles…'

'The biology of the Vispics certainly fascinates me,' admitted the Doctor. 'Their adult form is really quite something.' His voice suddenly dropped to the quietest of whispers. 'But don't take my word for it. See for yourself!'

Three large, unearthly creatures had just become

visible in the gloom up ahead. They each had a long, flattened body-shape, which broadened suddenly at both head and tail-end. Their hammer-headed, hammer-tailed bodies moved on six multi-jointed legs. Their fourth and foremost pair of limbs were hideously outsized, and ended in cruel, crescent-shaped claws.

The creatures' mid-sections still retained something of the bulbous maggoty shape of their larval form. But instead of blotched white, their bodies were now darker, and were covered all over in a strange shifting, multi-coloured sheen, like a film of oil on water.

One of the creatures was significantly larger than the other two. *Older, perhaps*, thought Amy, as she stared at the alien creatures. They were moving about under the dangling cocoons, as though patrolling.

'Keep very still!' the Doctor mouthed at her. 'They don't know we're here. Yet.'

'Great, I really *am* in a wildlife documentary,' Amy hissed back. 'How can you tell?'

'Because as soon as they *do* sense us, they'll attack. And there's a very obvious sign when that's about to happen.'

'Which is?'

To Amy's astonishment, the largest of the three adult Vispics suddenly disappeared. Completely.

'*That*!' cried the Doctor. 'Run!'

CHAPTER 10
A DEADLY BROOD

Amy and the Doctor covered the distance to the maintenance doorway a *lot* faster than on their outward trek. The adrenalin rush brought on by having a large alien predator chasing her worked wonders for Amy's girder-dodging skills. As she sprinted after the Doctor, she ducked, side-stepped and hurdled obstacles like an athlete.

Not far behind her, she could hear the clatter of many inhuman feet on concrete. There was the occasional ring of claw on metal – presumably the sound of the pursuing Vispic scrabbling over or squeezing through the steel supports of the grandstand's frame.

Amy glanced over her shoulder only once.

Despite the noises, there was nothing to see. She turned back, and kept running, heart pounding.

Then, thank goodness, there was the door. The Doctor narrowly beat her to it. He flung it open, bundled Amy through, then dived after her.

The light in the corridor was dazzling after the darkness under the stand. Screwing up her eyes against the glare, Amy helped the Doctor pull the maintenance door closed. He urgently applied his sonic screwdriver to the door's lock, to secure it.

An instant later, something heavy slammed into the other side of the door. Amy heard the sound of something sharp scrabbling and screeching against its inner surface for a few seconds. Then silence fell.

The Doctor, breathing heavily, leant his back against the door and slid down into a sitting position. He brushed his unruly hair, which was even wilder than ever after their mad dash, out of his eyes.

'Phew!' he gave Amy a broad grin. 'Invigorating stuff, eh, Pond? That's got my hearts pumping!'

Amy flopped down next to him. She was too busy trying to get her breath back to reply for a few moments.

'Do you think it's gone?' she said at last. She put her ear to the door. 'I can't hear anything.'

'I imagine it's returned to the cocoons,' said the Doctor. 'Its priority will be to protect them.'

'How did it just *vanish* like that?'

The Doctor gave her a smug look.

'I told you their biology was mightily impressive, Pond. Adult Vispics have remarkably sophisticated camouflage. They can adjust the pigmentation of every area of their skin. Change the colour of any part of their body at will.'

'Like a chameleon?'

'Like-*ish*,' said the Doctor. 'But a Vispic's ability to match its appearance to its background is *much* more advanced. Its sensory organs can pinpoint the exact position of any other living thing in its proximity. The Vispic analyses the precise background against which that particular observer is viewing it, then matches its skin pattern exactly to it – making itself more or less impossible to see.'

Amy looked thoughtful.

'But if their camouflage works like that, they could only hide themselves from one person at a time, couldn't they?' she asked. 'I mean, if two or three people were hanging around near a Vispic, they'd each see it against a different background, right? Depending on where they were. It couldn't blend in with *all* those backgrounds.'

'Clever girl, Pond. Absolutely right. If there are multiple observers near it, the Vispic has to try to take their different perspectives into account. It calculates the ideal camouflage pattern for each, then alternates between them, very, very quickly. Its camouflage becomes less effective. You'd be able to perceive its body – as a flickering area in your vision. The more people the Vispic tries to conceal itself from, the more skin patterns it has to cycle through, and the more obvious the flicker.'

'So, if you've got plenty of company, you've a chance of keeping track of where it's got to? But if it only has to hide itself from you, it can pretty much disappear?'

'Precisely.'

'So they're big, hungry and invisible.' Amy raised her eyebrows. 'Lovely. Remind me to add them to my Top Ten Favourite Aliens list.'

'Their only flaw as a predator is their modest speed,' the Doctor told her. 'They're not particularly quick on their feet. But if your prey can't see you, you don't have to be especially fast to make a kill.'

'But what are they doing at *Wembley*?' asked Amy.

'Vispics are parasites. They have only one motivation – to find hosts.'

'I meant, how did they get here?'

'In larval form, they have the ability to spatially displace themselves.'

Amy gave the Doctor a look.

'You're talking Time Lord again.'

'They can burrow through space,' the Doctor simplified. 'You saw one do it – under the stand. That larva was cutting a dimensional wormhole, to allow itself into Earth space. Spatial displacement.'

Amy remembered the glowing orange circle

in mid-air.

'It's how they live,' the Doctor continued. 'First, locate a food source – a host population from which they can drain neural energy. Then pupate. Wrap up snug in a cocoon, within feeding range of that population. From there, they soak up the energy they need to metamorphose. When they've fed enough to transform, they emerge, as carnivorous adults. The adults prey on what remains of the host population. They lay eggs, which hatch into larvae, and the cycle starts again.'

'Charming. Not great pets, then.'

'It's no surprise that the Vispics have discovered Earth at this particular point in her history,' said the Doctor. 'The Space Race is going flat out, driving technology forward. Rockets, probes, satellites – they're all taking off around now. Literally. Earth has just arrived on the galactic scene. And she's obviously attracted some unwelcome attention…'

'But why *Wembley*?' said Amy. 'It seems a pretty random place to choose.'

'The Vispic larvae are luck-suckers, remember.

They feed on euphoria and joy. Right now, this stadium is packed with tens of thousands of football fans, all eagerly anticipating that their nation is about to win the World Cup.'

The Doctor swept back his drooping fringe with long fingers.

'To a Vispic, the supporters' excitement probably smells like bacon frying. They've sensed an oncoming feast. If England win, the leech larvae will be in feeding range of thousands of deliriously happy fans. They'll gorge themselves. There'll be enough positive energy for every Vispic we saw cocooned under there to metamorphose into an adult.'

Amy didn't need the Doctor to tell her what would follow – what the horrific consequences of hundreds of hungry adult Vispics being let loose on the streets of London would be. It didn't bear thinking about.

'So, what do we do, Doctor? How do we stop that happening?'

The Doctor raised his eyebrows.

'Not sure yet.' His expression changed to a frown. 'What puzzles me is how so *many* larvae have come to displace themselves to the same location. It suggests that they're being *called*, somehow. And if that *is* the case...'

His voice trailed off as his nine-hundred-and-something-year-old mind wrestled with this latest catastrophic problem.

Amy, too, tried desperately to think of something.

'I see what you meant now,' she said, after a few moments. 'Back in the gents.'

'Hmm?'

'When you told Rory that there might be more important things than the World Cup at stake.'

The Doctor suddenly leapt to his feet and gave an excited whoop.

'That's it! Of *course*! The *cup*!' He looked down at the startled Amy, his eyes alight. 'Pond – we *have* to get our hands on that trophy! Come on!'

And without further explanation, he sprinted away along the corridor.

Amy hauled herself to her feet, scowling.

'Not *you* as well?' she grumbled. 'It's bad enough having a soccer-obsessed husband. What is it with boys? It's only a stupid *game*...'

With a long-suffering sigh, she set off to catch up with the Doctor.

CHAPTER 11
HALF-TIME

To Rory's great astonishment and relief, he had made it through the first half without being rumbled.

He had fully expected to make a howler of a touchline decision at some point, which would expose him as an impostor. He had also worried that forty-five minutes of the shimmer's sickening side-effects might prove too much for him. But thankfully, neither of these fears had come true.

In fact, he had been rather fortunate so far in the way the match had unfolded. There had been little need for either linesman to get involved. West Germany's early goal, in the twelfth minute, had been at Rory's end of the pitch. Helmut Haller had fired in his shot after England's usually rock-solid left-back Ray Wilson had failed to clear a German cross. But as there was no suggestion of offside, the referee had awarded the goal without having to consult Rory. Hurst had equalised for England six minutes later, at the other end of the pitch – which was the other linesman's area of responsibility. Apart from a handful of relatively straightforward throw-in decisions, when Rory had only needed to flag for whose throw it was, he had thankfully had little to do.

The half-time scoreline of 1-1 meant that so far, at least, the match was still on track – despite Bakhramov's absence. But Rory knew he wasn't out of the woods yet. Not by a long way. He still had to survive another full hour of play – and nausea – before he could make the all-important goal line decision. Only that would guarantee England's victory, and prevent history from unravelling.

But right now, he had a more immediate challenge. He had to get through the half-time interval without blowing his cover.

When the referee's whistle blast signalled the end of the first forty-five minutes, Rory didn't hang around. He made sure he was the first of the three match officials to leave the pitch, and swiftly headed for their private changing rooms. Once there, he immediately locked himself in a toilet cubicle and deactivated his shimmer.

The relief was immediate and immense. For the first time in nearly an hour, Rory didn't feel as though he was about to throw up.

He sat on the toilet, with its lid down, enjoying a few minutes of normal-feeling insides, and hoping to stay well out of everyone's way until he could return to the touchline for the second half.

Ten minutes or so passed. Rory didn't hear anybody else enter the changing room. Perhaps the referee and Czech linesman wouldn't need to use it during the interval. That would suit him just fine.

Hiding in the cubicle was giving Rory the slight creeps. After all, it was in the cubicle next door that he had found the dead man only an hour ago.

Rory had purposefully *not* shut himself in *there*.

He wondered if the Doctor and Amy had made any progress figuring out what had happened to the poor man. He wondered, too, where they had decided to hide the real Bakhramov till he awoke; and whether they had managed to catch any of the first half of the match.

His thoughts were interrupted by the clatter of studs on the concrete floor. The noise rose to a crescendo, then began to fade. The players had passed the changing room, heading back to the tunnel for the second half.

When he was confident that the last player had gone by, Rory emerged from the toilet cubicle and slipped out into the corridor, planning to follow the players back out onto the pitch at a discreet distance.

'What are you doing down here, young man?'

Rory spun round guiltily. He found himself face to face with a middle-aged gentleman in a pale blue tracksuit with red-white-and-blue cuffs. Rory recognised the man's stern face instantly.

He had seen many photographs of it in football memorabilia and magazines. It belonged to Alf Ramsey, the England team manager.

Heart pounding, Rory groped hopelessly for a reply.

'You're not one of the match officials,' growled Ramsey, before Rory could think of what to say. 'What business have you got in their changing rooms?'

An alarm sounded somewhere in Rory's brain. Why didn't Ramsey recognise him as Bakhramov, the linesman?

His heart sank. He had forgotten to turn the shimmer back on.

'Ah! I... er...' stammered Rory, now completely flustered. 'I'm one of the *reserve* officials!'

'Reserve officials?' This role was clearly new to the England boss.

'Uh-huh, yeah,' Rory blundered on. 'Er... you know... in case any of the original three need substituting?' he suggested hopefully.

Ramsey continued to glare at him suspiciously.

'New FOOFA rules,' Rory explained. 'To ensure fair play...'

Ramsey's frown deepened. 'Foofa?'

'That's right!' Rory was floundering. 'Anyway... enough about me!' He tried desperately to change the subject. 'How do *you* feel the game is going so far, Mr Ramsey?' He smiled innocently. 'England Manager. Sir.'

Ramsey raised his eyebrows.

'Could be worse,' he growled. 'Although we made a bad defensive error to allow their goal.'

'Just a blip though, wasn't it?' said Rory encouragingly. 'I wouldn't worry. I'm sure your back four will play an absolute blinder for the rest of the match.'

'You think so, hmm?'

'I do, sir. I *know* so. Trust me.'

A crazy idea suddenly popped into Rory's head. After the many hours he had spent playing FIFA 11 and Football Manager, he liked to think he knew a thing or two about getting the best out of a team. And here was the only opportunity he was ever likely to have to influence a *real* soccer manager. And not just *any* manager. The most famous English coach in history.

'I wonder, Mr Ramsey, sir... might I make a suggestion?'

'Go on.'

'It's just... well, watching the first half, sir, it crossed my mind that we might give their centre-backs a bit more trouble if you told Ball to use that near-post cross of his more. He's on fire today.'

Ramsey fixed Rory with a severe look for a few unnerving moments. Rory was beginning to realise that the England manager didn't really do other kinds of look.

'Interesting suggestion, young man,' said Ramsey at last. 'You might even have a point. Now – if you'll excuse me, I have a World Cup team to coach...'

Rory hastily stepped aside, with an awkward half bow. He watched Ramsey move away towards the players' tunnel, and let out a huge sigh of relief. That had been a *very* close shave. And what was he thinking, giving the England manager tactical tips?

He ducked back inside the changing room, and quickly twisted the dial casing on the shimmer to reactivate it. The now-familiar sickening ache once more gripped his stomach. He glanced across at the mirror above the sink – and saw Tofik Bakhramov staring palely back at him.

Daring to delay no further, Rory dived back out into the corridor and hurried after Ramsey and his players, ready – or as ready as he would ever be – for the second half.

CHAPTER 12
BOMB SCARE

'Nearly there, Pond!' puffed the Doctor. 'Just up ahead, on the left!'

The Doctor and Amy were still running – back along the stadium corridor. It was the one they had followed earlier, which led past the room in which they had spied the Jules Rimet Trophy.

'There's someone coming out!' replied Amy. 'Look!'

They both came to a standstill. Twenty metres along the corridor, a group of four police officers had just emerged from the Press Room door. They were the men they had seen earlier, guarding the trophy. One of them had it with him now, carrying it carefully in its glass case.

The police party began making its way in the

opposite direction to where Amy and the Doctor stood.

'Excuse me! Hello there!'

All four policemen looked round in surprise at the Doctor's shout. As he quickly strode forward to join them, he slipped his hand into his inside jacket pocket. He muttered a quiet aside to Amy.

'About time you and I had a career change, don't you think, Pond? Been with FOOFA long enough.' He pulled out his psychic paper. 'How do you fancy being a plain-clothes police officer?'

Amy snorted. 'There's nothing "plain" about *your* clothes, mister braces and bow tie,' she whispered back.

'Hello, hello!' said the Doctor cheerily, as he and Amy approached. He grinned. 'Or should that be *'ello, 'ello, 'ello*?' He hooked his thumbs in his braces, and bent both knees to bob up and down.

The four police officers glared at him. Not one showed even a trace of a smile.

'Just kidding. You know. Classic bobby-on-the-beat thing...' persevered the Doctor, still smiling. 'No?'

The nearest policeman stepped forward. The shoulders of his uniform bore the triple chevrons of a sergeant. He was clearly in charge.

'How can we help you, sir?' The sergeant's tone was rather severe.

'The name's Lineker. Agent Lineker,' replied the Doctor. 'From Metropolitan Special Branch.' He held out his psychic paper for inspection. The sergeant peered at it warily.

'This is my colleague, Agent Beckham.' The Doctor gestured to Amy. She gave the officers a solemn nod.

The sergeant's suspicious gaze was still fixed on the psychic paper. Finally he looked back at the Doctor.

'*You're* with Special Branch?' he said, raising his eyebrows.

'Indeed, sergeant. Plain clothes.'

Amy cleared her throat.

'And what can we do for you, Agent Lineker?' asked the sergeant.

The Doctor extended one of his long fingers.

'I'd be terribly grateful if I could borrow that trophy you've got there.'

The sergeant frowned.

'Can't let you do that, sir, I'm afraid. I'm under strict orders to see that it gets to the Royal Box safely. Her Majesty is to present it at the end of the match. I was told not to let it out of my sight. I'm sure you understand, sir – after the recent theft, and all.'

The Doctor tucked away his psychic paper, then clapped a hand on the sergeant's shoulder.

'Absolutely, sergeant. And you won't have to. Let it out of your sight, I mean. I just need to take a quick look at it. But it is rather important that I examine the cup *before* it comes into the Queen's proximity.'

'And why would that be, sir?'

'Because, sergeant, we have reason to believe it's a bomb.'

All four policemen looked understandably alarmed.

'A *bomb*?'

'That's right. As you say, the trophy went

missing recently. Special Branch has been looking into exactly who took it. We've just uncovered evidence that it was stolen – and then returned – by a known anti-royal terrorist. One Rory "The Wrecker" Williams. Very nasty piece of work. Show them, Beckham.'

Amy was a little caught out. She hastily dug out her mobile phone, and used its touch-sensitive screen to open up her photo library. She filtered the library for images of Rory. It didn't take her long to find a pretty grim head-and-shoulders photo of him. Boy, did she remember *that* party...

Amy selected the photo for full-screen display, and held up her phone for the sergeant to see.

All four officers had watched the entire process open-mouthed. None of them had ever dreamt of, let alone seen, technology like this. To the nineteen-sixties mind, Amy's twenty-first century phone was about as jaw-dropping as pure magic. Which, Amy realised, was precisely why the Doctor had suggested she use it. In the eyes of the four policemen, such incredible technology could only have been issued by Special Branch. They now bought the Doctor's story hook, line and sinker.

'Williams is a genius with explosives,' the Doctor continued. 'And he has something against the Royal Family. We've already foiled one attempt on Prince Philip's life. Nasty business with a rigged polo saddle. We believe Williams has booby-trapped the World Cup trophy, knowing that it's to be presented by Her Majesty.'

'Really, sir?' The sergeant was gripped now. 'We can't have that, sir!'

'No sergeant, we can't,' agreed the Doctor earnestly. 'So if I could just take a quick look...'

At the sergeant's signal, the officer holding the cased trophy hurriedly passed it over to the Doctor. The constable looked rather relieved. He had been a little fidgety ever since the mention of the word "bomb".

'Now then...' muttered the Doctor, placing the case gently on the corridor floor.

He took out his sonic screwdriver, then knelt down to apply it to the lock on the case's lid. The lock immediately released.

The four policemen looked on in amazement. This lock-cracking gadget was obviously another piece of Special Branch techno-wizardry.

The Doctor lifted the heavy trophy from the case. He began scanning its golden surface with his sonic screwdriver's glowing green tip.

He turned the trophy over. As he did so, it momentarily slipped in his grasp. All four police officers flinched visibly. The Doctor grinned at them.

'Whoops!'

He turned his attention to the roughly cubic block of lapis lazuli that formed the base of the trophy. As he scanned its underside, the sonic flickered more brightly.

'Ah-ha!'

The Doctor fiddled with the sonic screwdriver's controls, then applied it once more to the exact centre of the lapis lazuli. Very slowly, he began to draw the sonic's tip away.

Amy watched in amazement. Something thin

and pale pink was gradually emerging from the trophy's base, as though drawn out by the pull of the sonic. It was a spiralling filament, covered in tiny frill-like swirls. It was made of a translucent, coral-coloured material. In fact, that was what it most reminded Amy of – coral. A long, slender spiral of fragile coral.

'What's *that*?' she asked, before thinking.

The Doctor flashed her a look. He carefully drew out another few centimetres of the whatever-it-was. Its end finally emerged from the trophy base, leaving no trace of a hole. The Doctor caught it as it came free and passed it to Amy.

'High explosive strand, Beckham,' he said gravely, with a discreet wink. 'As we suspected. Complete with detonator. Very hi-tech. This Williams monster knows his stuff.'

The Doctor stood up and tucked his sonic screwdriver back in his pocket.

'There! All done!'

Without warning, he casually tossed the trophy towards the police officer who had originally held it. Fortunately, the constable had good reactions. He caught the hefty gold cup, staring at it like it was a live grenade.

'No need to worry!' the Doctor reassured him. 'It won't harm anyone now! Completely defused. You can pop it back it its case, and get it over to the Royal Box for the presentation as planned.'

He turned to the sergeant.

'And I'd appreciate it if we could keep this little incident to ourselves, yes? National security, and all that.'

He turned to Amy.

'Come, Agent Beckham!' He gestured to the nearby open doorway. 'You and I have important Special Branch type things to discuss.'

'Right.' Amy nodded. 'Absolutely.' She led the way into the Press Room, still holding the strange coral-like strand.

The Doctor gave the four dumbstruck police officers a final broad smile, then followed, closing the door behind him.

There was a long silence in the corridor.

'Sarge?' The youngest officer was first to speak. 'How hard is it to get into Special Branch?'

CHAPTER 13
THE BIG PROBLEM

'So, Agent Lineker – what does this thing *really* do?'

Amy was examining the peculiar coral-like filament that the Doctor had just extracted from the base of the Jules Rimet Trophy. The two of them were alone in the Press Room.

'It's a displacement anchor,' replied the Doctor. 'Acts as both a beacon and a fixing point for the Vispic larvae. It's what's calling them all here, to Wembley. And it serves as a secure anchorage once they get here.'

'You make it sound like they're having to cling on.'

'They are, in a way. Displacing yourself isn't

easy. There are strong forces acting to keep you at your point of origin. The Vispics can override those forces if they have a sufficiently secure displacement anchor to fix onto, in their target location. That's what you're holding.'

'But where did it come from?'

'The first Vispic to burrow a wormhole into Earth space must have managed to do so unassisted. Probably the one that turned into the larger adult we saw. It must have set up that anchor so that others could follow.'

'But it was *inside the World Cup*,' said Amy. 'I mean, that's a bit weird, isn't it? Why there?'

'Think about it, Amy,' said the Doctor. 'What better place could there be? By its very nature, the trophy is always a focus for celebration and joy. Winning the World Cup creates mass euphoria among the fans of the winning nation. And the trophy is at the heart of that upsurge of good feeling. Exactly where a hungry luck-sucking larva would choose to be.'

The Doctor settled on the edge of the table.

'Rory's whole trophy-theft story struck me as odd right away. Why did the cup turn up again? Any thief capable of stealing it in the first place would hardly have been so inept as to leave it lying in a hedge. Unless of course they *intended* it to be recovered.'

Amy didn't look like she was keeping up.

'The police never did manage to track down the culprit. But then they were looking for a *human*...'

The penny dropped.

'You mean – that adult Vispic took it?' Amy looked at the filament. 'To put this inside?'

The Doctor nodded.

'I don't wish to take any credit away from our canine hero Pickles, but it was part of the Vispic plan that the trophy should be "found". It was a simple way to ensure the trophy returned to the centre of World Cup activity – with the displacement anchor concealed inside.'

The Doctor put out a hand for the anchor. Amy passed it to him. He took out his sonic screwdriver, and gave the filament a quick once-over.

'Their plan's worked a treat, too, hasn't it?' said Amy grimly. 'All those larvae under the stands, ready and waiting for the fans to go crazy, so they can suck all the happiness out of them…'

'Don't throw in the towel just yet, Pond!' The Doctor tucked his sonic away and slid off the tabletop. He began pacing the floor, twirling the strange frilled strand like a majorette's baton. 'This thing may be the reason so many Vispics have found their way here, but it *might* offer us a way of sending them packing, too.'

'How?'

'As I said, there are forces that act to resist an organism displacing itself. A strong pull back towards the point of origin – a bit like being attached to where you set out from by a piece of elastic. While the Vispics have a secure anchor point…' – he waggled the filament at her – '… they can withstand that pull. But if we were to *destroy* it…'

'*Twang*!' cried Amy excitedly.

'Exactly. No more Vispics. The whole host of larvae and adults would be instantly drawn back to their original location.'

The Doctor stopped pacing, held up the filament, and stared at it searchingly.

'This is the key to the Vispics' scheme, but also its weakness. Another reason, I imagine, why they hid it so well.'

'So what are we waiting for?' asked Amy. 'Let's smash it up!'

'Be my guest.'

The Doctor tossed the filament back to Amy. She took hold of it by its ends, and attempted to snap it in two. She gritted her teeth, and tried harder. But despite its fragile appearance, the slim strand wouldn't break.

Amy decided to get serious. She dragged a table across from against the Press Room wall, and positioned it next to the one in the centre of the room, leaving a narrow gap between them. Then she laid the filament across the gap. She picked up a sturdy wooden chair, lifted it over her head, and brought it crashing down.

The chair disintegrated, splintering into a

twisted mess. Amy yelled as the jolt jarred her upper body. She dropped what was left of the chair. The filament lay on the floor, entirely undamaged.

Amy glared at the Doctor, red-faced.

'I'm not going to be able to break it, am I?'

The Doctor shook his head.

'You knew that already, didn't you?' said Amy.

The Doctor nodded. He reached down to pick up the displacement anchor. He closed one eye and squinted along its length, first from one end, then the other.

'That, Pond, is our big problem. How to unmake it. It appears to be built around a molecular core of Paratraxium. Almost indestructible.'

'Almost?'

The Doctor hesitated.

'I can think of two ways in which it *might* be destroyed,' he told Amy.

'Go on.'

'The first would involve subjecting it to a *very* high temperature. The sort generated near the Earth's core, or at the heart of an erupting volcano.'

'Not a *great* option, that one, is it?' said Amy drily. 'I'm guessing there's not a lot of volcanic activity in north-west London right now. What's Plan B?'

'To run a powerful electric pulse through it,' said the Doctor. 'Paratraxium has an extremely high electrical resistance. If the voltage was sufficient, it should cause the core to heat up beyond its tolerance.'

'*Now* you're talking. Electricity we have – even in the sixties.'

'Not at the sort of voltage we'd need. It would take over a hundred thousand volts. No part of London's city grid carries that sort of flow.'

'Isn't there any other way?'

The Doctor shook his head. But Amy wasn't having it.

'There must be *something* we can do!' she insisted. 'We can't just sit around and wait for half the population of London to go down the tube…'

The Doctor's face lit up. He seized Amy by the shoulders.

'Pond, you're a genius! You've done it again!'

'What?' Amy looked confused.

'That's the answer! The *Tube*!' cried the Doctor. 'The London Underground! The whole track is electrified!'

'You think we might be able to fry this thing by hooking it up to a Tube line?'

'Not directly, no. The electrified track probably carries about a thousand volts of direct current, at most. One kilovolt isn't enough. But there *must* be some way to amplify it...'

The Doctor began pacing back and forth once more, running his hands through his hair as he tried to think.

'Wembley's entire roof is supported on an aluminium framework. I might be able to multi-loop the electric flow through *that*. Create a makeshift step-up transformer. Boost the voltage. We'd need to run it through an inverter first, to get an *alternating* current...'

The Doctor was taking shorter and shorter circuits.

'It *could* work! If I get the roof-loop right, we should be able to create a powerful enough electric pulse to disintegrate the Paratraxium core!'

'Then bye-bye luck-suckers!' enthused Amy. 'Brilliant!'

'I'd have to isolate the stands themselves, of course…'

'Or?'

'Or 93,000 football fans will get a nasty shock,' said the Doctor. 'Literally.'

Amy looked concerned. 'Okay… feeling *slightly* less enthusiastic now…'

'And it'll take me a little while to set up.' He stopped pacing, and looked at Amy, his eyes alive. 'I'll need *you* to make the connection to the Underground system.'

''Course you will. And that'll involve more running, presumably?'

'Possibly a *little*, Pond,' admitted the Doctor.

He flashed her a grin.

'But probably a lot.'

CHAPTER 14
COME ON, ENGLAND!

Out on the Wembley pitch, both teams were giving it everything they had. There were only three or four minutes of normal time left to play. England were a goal up.

The teams had been locked in a 1-1 stalemate for most of the gruelling second half. Then, in the seventy-eighth minute, England had finally broken the deadlock. They had snatched a crucial second goal. It had come from an Alan Ball cross – much to Rory's delight. Ball had delivered his corner-kick to Hurst, whose deflected shot had fallen kindly for his West Ham team mate, Martin Peters.

As Peters' close range shot hit the back of the

German net, Rory, watching from the touchline, had let out a triumphant whoop. A split second later, he had remembered who he was supposed to be. A neutral, unbiased official. He had hastily tried to disguise his delighted reaction as a fit of energetic coughing.

He needn't have bothered. The watching fans weren't interested in the linesman's rather peculiar behaviour. They were too busy either screaming their heads off with delight, or hanging them in despair.

Since then, West Germany had been doing everything in their power to save the match. A goal down, with time running out, they had pushed everyone forward. They were mounting attack after attack on the English goal.

But England, too, were digging deep. The players were defending valiantly, determined not to concede a goal. They knew that a famous victory was within their reach. The World Cup would be theirs if they could hold on for just a few more minutes.

The English fans in the packed stands were in an agony of expectation. One moment they were cheering wildly as Nobby Stiles made yet another vital tackle; the next they were gasping with relief as Gordon Banks just managed to punch away a fierce German shot. The trophy was *so* nearly in their grasp…

No one was more on edge than Rory. He was finding the suspense almost as unbearable as the stomach-churning effect of the shimmer. He was beginning to regret wishing that history should follow its familiar course. That would mean the match going into extra time. Another thirty minutes of play. Rory wasn't sure he could hold it together that long.

Maybe the Germans won't equalise, he thought hopefully.

Despite his many TARDIS trips, Rory still struggled with the whole re-living history thing. Time travel did his head in, full stop – but particularly going *back* in time. Was it inevitable that events on the pitch would follow the pattern he knew? Or not? Perhaps a straightforward 2-1 win for England was still a possibility. Maybe *this* time around, there would be no extra time, no controversial goal line decision to make…

Another tremendous roar went up from the crowd as Banks claimed the ball from a dangerous German cross. The England goalkeeper was playing out of his skin.

The crowd had been brilliant, too. The rousing support from the England fans had been constant throughout the match. The atmosphere was fantastic. No one was crazier for football than the English.

It struck Rory – not for the first time – as a great shame that England hadn't hosted a World Cup in *his* lifetime. He knew that during the time he had been travelling with the Doctor, the Football Association had tried once again to bring the tournament to English turf. He had pinned his hopes on their bid to stage the 2018 tournament. But it hadn't come off. Wembley wouldn't see another match like this in a *very* long time.

Rory's thoughts were brought back to the

here and now by another loud outburst from the crowd. This time, it was a collective groan from the England fans. The referee had awarded West Germany a free kick, just outside the English penalty box. Jack Charlton had been penalised for a foul on the German captain, Seeler.

The match was now into its final minute. But there was still time for the Germans to ruin the English party.

The teams had changed ends for the second half, which meant the English goal was now at the end of the pitch furthest from Rory. He watched anxiously from a distance, as West German winger Lothar Emmerich lined up to take the kick. The volume of the crowd fell dramatically, as thousands of English fans held their breath.

Rory remembered this free kick only too well. It looked likely that history *was* about to repeat itself – or replay itself? – after all.

Sure enough, moments later, Wolfgang Weber was streaking away from the English goal, arms aloft in celebration. Emmerich's kick had been bravely blocked, but the deflected ball had fallen for Weber, rushing in at the far post. His close-range shot had given Banks no chance. The Germans had equalised within the dying seconds of normal time.

Rory glumly looked up at the scoreboard. It was mounted on a rather precarious-looking balcony, jutting out from under the stadium's west-end roof, to Rory's right. It showed the team names and scores in white text on a black background. Two men in white coats were perched on the gallery that ran behind it. It was their job to manually change the giant numerals that made up the scoreline display.

Rory watched one of the scoreboard officials replace the "1" next to "Germany W." with a large "2" – and heard the referee's whistle blow for the end of normal time. He looked over his shoulder at the North Stand, which had fallen very quiet. The England fans were looking shell-shocked, stunned by this last-gasp German goal. Rory looked back across row upon row of dismayed faces.

He did a double-take. For a moment, he was

almost *sure* he had caught sight of a figure running across the North Stand roof. A very familiar figure.

Rory shook his head to clear it. The shimmer must be messing with his vision. He looked up again.

No, there was nobody up there. His eyes were playing tricks.

Why would the Doctor have been on the roof, anyway?

Rory turned his attention back to the pitch. The England and West Germany players were making the most of the short interval before extra time, taking the opportunity to rest and stretch-off. They would be hoping to stave off cramp and somehow coax another thirty minutes of running out of their tired legs.

I've got to hang in there, too, thought Rory determinedly. He mustn't let his concentration falter now, however grim the shimmer was making him feel. Once extra time kicked off, he would need to be on his toes. His big moment – Hurst's controversial second goal – was fast approaching.

And if I don't get things exactly right in the next

thirty minutes, he thought anxiously, *it could all be over for England.*

Though Rory could not have known it, at that very moment, up on the North Stand roof, the Doctor was thinking exactly the same thing.

CHAPTER 15
THE WRONG TARDIS

Amy sprinted north along Olympic Way, heart pounding. For the umpteenth time, she checked over her shoulder. Since leaving the stadium, she hadn't been able to shake off the feeling that someone – or some*thing* – was following her. But as far as she could tell, she was still alone.

She didn't slacken her pace. Even if she wasn't being pursued – for a change – she was still up against the clock. The Doctor's plan would only work if they could put it into action before the Vispic larvae transformed. Which meant they only had until the end of the match. Time was running out fast.

Amy reached the junction with Fulton Road

and turned right onto its south-side pavement. The main road, which had been so busy earlier, was now deserted. Her route along Olympic Way had been eerily quiet, too. Anyone who wasn't actually at the match was tucked away inside somewhere, following it on radio – or, if they were lucky enough to have access to one, watching on TV. London's streets had never been so empty.

Amy jogged along the pavement, then crossed to the other side of the road. She passed the news-stand where she, Rory and the Doctor had stopped off earlier. It was locked up and unattended.

She was beginning to get a stitch. But it wasn't far now. Albion Way, where the TARDIS had materialised, was just up ahead. She put on a last effort to keep up her speed, determined not to let the Doctor down…

PC Sanderson's good intentions of listening to 'some' of the match hadn't quite worked out. The game was now in its ninetieth minute, and the young policeman was still shut away in his call box, listening intently to the gripping commentary on his borrowed radio.

'...and as Emmerich strides forward to take this last-ditch free kick, a nervous silence has fallen over the England fans...'

'Miss it, miss it, miss it...' muttered Sanderson. He was perched on the edge of the box's bench seat, with a forgotten cup of cold tea in his hand.

'...Emmerich's shot is blocked by Cohen and – oh! Dear me! It's a goal! Weber scores for Germany!'

'NO!' Sanderson let out a groan of despair and slumped back against the wall of the box.

'There are appeals from the English players for handball! But the referee waves away their protests! The goal stands. The West German centre-back has snatched a last-minute equaliser...'

He couldn't believe what he was hearing. How could they have let them score *now*, when they were *so* close?

'...and there's the whistle to signal the end of the second half! So, it's all square at 2-2! Both teams will need to summon the energy to play another thirty

minutes, to decide this epic contest. England, who only moments ago seemed destined to lift the World Cup here at Wembley, now find themselves still with everything to do to win th–'

Suddenly, Sanderson stood bolt upright, spilling his tea. Someone had just burst through the door of the police box.

It was a pretty young woman with long red hair. She was breathing fast. She looked as surprised to see Sanderson as he was to see her.

'Ah…' She looked around the box's cramped interior as though it wasn't what she had expected to find. 'Sorry… my… mistake…' she panted. 'Wrong TARDIS!'

She took another second or two to get her breath. Sanderson was still too taken aback to speak.

The stranger flashed a smile at him. 'Sorry if I startled you, officer.' She glanced at the radio set, which was still chattering away. 'Been following the match?'

Sanderson looked a little sheepish.

'I was… erm… just listening to a few minutes, yes, miss.'

'How's it going?'

'Not well. It looked like we had it won, but the Germans just equalised. It's going to extra time.'

The stranger looked delighted.

'Yes!'

Sanderson frowned. He failed to see how Germany scoring could be good news.

'But surely you don't want *them* to win?'

'No,' said the redhead. 'No, I don't want Germany to win. I don't want *anyone* to win just yet. Extra time is absolutely what we need.'

Sanderson was finding this unexpected conversation increasingly confusing. He decided to start again.

'May I ask your name, miss?'

'You go first.'

'Very well. PC Sanderson, of Harlesden Police Station, at your service.'

'First name?'

'William. Bill.'

This wasn't going as Sanderson had intended. Somehow, *he* seemed to have ended up answering the questions.

'Bill.' The girl smiled. 'As in "the old Bill". Good name for a copper. That and "Bobby".'

Sanderson once again tried to take charge.

'And you are?'

In response, the young woman pulled a slim, shiny, rectangular object from her pocket. She stared at its smooth surface for a moment, stroking and tapping it several times with her finger. Sanderson was amazed to see tiny luminous pictures flit across the device's glassy face. The girl held it up in front of him.

'Agent Beckham, Special Branch.'

Sanderson stared in disbelief. It was a miniature display screen, not altogether unlike a tiny television. It showed a picture of the redhead's face, with the text "My Profile" above it. There was more text underneath. But before he could read it, the young woman withdrew her hand.

'What... what *is* that thing?' stammered

Sanderson. 'It's amazing!'

'Standard issue Special Branch equipment.'

'So, you're with the Met? Like me?'

'Uh-huh. But plain clothes, assigned to anti-terrorist stuff.' She moved closer to address him earnestly. 'We have a serious situation on our hands, PC Bill Sanderson. A Code Thirteen.'

'Code Thirteen?'

'Extra-terrestrial invasion,' stated the young woman, without flinching. 'How do you fancy helping to save the population of London, Bill?'

'Extra-terrestrial inva–' Sanderson pulled a face. 'Is this some kind of joke, miss?'

The young woman's expression didn't falter. She was deadly serious, he could see.

'You're suggesting... *aliens*?' said Sanderson. 'But that's not possible!' He hesitated. 'Is it?' The magical technology the young constable had just seen in action had turned his idea of what was "possible" upside down. 'I mean, they don't exist, do they?'

'Oh yeah. They exist all right. And right now

they're out and about here, in London. Big scary people-eating ones. And I could use a little help dealing with them.'

Sanderson was finding this surprise meeting most unsettling. Once again, he tried to get a grip.

'You say you're from Special Branch?'

The young woman nodded.

'Were *they* behind setting up that second call box?' asked Sanderson. 'The one next to this one? Has that got something to do with all this?'

Agent Beckham's eyes lit up.

'It *has*, Sanderson. Smart guess. And a quick look inside there should change your mind about the whole "impossible" thing.' She turned back towards the open door. 'Come on – I'll show you around.'

The bewildered police officer found the idea of being "shown around" a five-foot-square box slightly odd. But nothing about this meeting had been anything *but* odd. Deciding to save his questions for the time being, he followed the young woman out of the police box door.

Amy watched PC Sanderson's face as he struggled to take in his surroundings. She remembered her own first reaction to the TARDIS's mind-bending interior. Sanderson was going through the same sequence of emotions – total shock, shifting to amazed delight, then on to utter bafflement.

'But…'

His voice trailed off. He continued to gawp uncomprehendingly at the vast cavern-like interior of the Time Lord craft.

Amy grinned at him.

'Loopy, isn't it? Bet you never realised Special Branch was *that* special!'

She hurried up the ramp towards the central circular platform, then made her way around the console, to her left, peering down at the floor.

'Now then… third segment round, clockwise, from the ramp. That's what the Doctor said. One… two… *three*!' She dropped to her knees beside a rectangular panel in the floor. 'Top left corner…' muttered Amy, reaching across it. She made a fist, and gave the floor a good hard thump.

The opposite ends of the panel suddenly seemed to shrink back slightly, and its surface became scored with narrow concertina folds. Amy slipped her hand into the gap that had appeared at one edge. She slid the panel aside to reveal a crammed storage hatch below.

Amy hastily began rummaging through the hatch's contents. She lifted out a strange contraption that looked like someone had covered a small fire extinguisher with sink-plunger suction cups. Amy laid it to one side, then fished out another equally bizarre-looking piece of equipment. Then another. And another.

'Who's the Doctor?'

Sanderson was still staring about, wide-eyed. But he had regained the ability to speak, at least.

'Er, a fellow Special Branch officer,' Amy replied, without leaving off her search. 'Agent Lineker. *What* is *that*?' She impatiently cast aside yet another peculiar device. 'He's running this operation. "The Doctor" is sort of a codename.'

'Right,' the constable nodded numbly.

'He's our Code Thirteen expert,' Amy went on. 'Knows loads about aliens and stuff.'

'I see.'

As she drew her next find from the hatch, Amy gave a triumphant cry.

'Gotcha!'

She was holding a pair of very large crocodile clips, locked together by their sprung jaws. They had handle-grips made of colourful rubbery material. Both had one red handle, and one yellow.

Amy got to her feet, and hurried back down the ramp.

'What are they?' asked PC Sanderson.

'Connectors. Together they're a "cordless extension lead" apparently. The Doctor – Agent Lineker, I mean – thinks they might help us with the save-the-city thing.'

'How?'

Amy made for the TARDIS door.

'I'll explain on the way there.'

'Where?'

Sanderson followed her, back out onto the

pavement of Albion Way. He was beginning to feel embarrassed by his own aimless-sounding one-word questions.

'Wembley Park Tube station,' Amy told him. 'We need to get there as fast as possible. Which is where I was hoping you might be able to help. Do you have a bicycle I could use?'

'Not a *pedal* bike, no,' said Sanderson. 'But I could take you there on the back of my patrol bike…'

He quickly led Amy round the back of his own police box. Parked against the kerb was a gleaming black motorcycle. It was a 650cc Triumph Thunderbird, the standard patrol bike of the Metropolitan force, and Sanderson's pride and joy.

'Would that do?'

Amy looked at the immaculate motorcycle admiringly. It was a truly classic machine. As a teenager, Amy had had a poster on her bedroom wall of a young Marlon Brando – in her opinion *the* most gorgeous male movie star of all time.

It had been taken from the film *The Wild One*. Brando was sitting astride a bike just like this one.

Amy gave Sanderson a broad grin.

'*Absolutely*, constable,' she purred. 'That'll do very nicely indeed.'

CHAPTER 16
GOALSKY!

Rory checked his watch. Not the fake Vinvocci wristwatch – which he was beginning to hate with all his heart – but his own, ordinary, non-stomach-churning one.

Nine minutes of extra time were almost up. Rory knew Geoff Hurst would score his controversial goal in the eleventh minute. That meant he had little over sixty seconds before his big moment arrived. Then it would be up to him to make sure the vital goal counted.

To his horror, Rory suddenly realised that so far, he had given no thought as to *how*. How would he communicate his decision that the goal should stand? He knew from watching old TV footage of the famous match that after Hurst's shot, the referee came running over to the touchline to consult Bakhramov. What was he going to do when that happened?

Should he have prepared something to say? In Russian?

Presumably, thought Rory, Bakhramov must have said something like "Yes, it *was* a goal," when the referee asked his opinion – even if the Swiss official didn't understand the linesman's exact words.

But what on Earth was that in Russian?

Rory's mind raced. His knowledge of the Russian language was almost non-existent. What little he knew he had picked up from watching old spy films, which often had a Russian character as the criminal mastermind. Rory recalled a scene in an early James Bond movie, in which a cold-hearted Russian villain refused to listen to reason. What did the baddy say as he shook his head mercilessly?

"*Nyet*". That was it. So "nyet" was "no". But

what was "yes"?

Rory tried to picture the same Bond villain giving orders to his band of armed heavies. What was it they grunted as they nodded obediently?

"*Da*". Of course! "Yes" was "da", he was sure.

As for the "it was a goal" bit, he would just have to wing it. If he made up some Russian-sounding words, maybe the referee wouldn't notice they weren't genuine. A lot of Russian names ended in "-ov" or "-sky", didn't they? He could include a few of those endings in whatever he said...

Rory's attention was drawn back to the game. Alan Ball had just sprinted past right in front of him, chasing the ball down the right wing. Rory could see the two English centre-forwards, Hurst and Hunt, hurrying forward in support. He recognised the shape of this attacking move from the many, many times he had seen these particular seconds of play before – and knew the time for planning was over.

This was it.

Ball whipped in a short cross to the near side of

the German penalty box. Hurst had found space to receive it. He controlled the ball with his first touch, then span towards the goal and fired in a fierce, rising shot. It rocketed over the flat-capped head of the West German keeper, Tilkowski.

The ball hit the midpoint of the crossbar, hard. It ricocheted off the underside of the bar, straight downwards, and struck the ground between the German goalposts.

The deflection off the bar had set the ball spinning fiercely. The spin caused it to bounce up at an angle, out of the goalmouth. A desperate German defender headed the ball over his own goal, to put it out of play.

But the English players were already celebrating. They ran to congratulate Hurst, convinced that his shot had crossed the goal line, and that he had just put them ahead.

The West Germans felt otherwise. Rory watched them surround the referee, protesting. The Swiss official waved them away, then began to make his way across the pitch towards Rory.

One thing Rory had never expected was that when the time came, he would be in any doubt as to whether he was doing the *fair* thing. To his own astonishment, after witnessing the Hurst goal first-hand, he was a tiny bit uneasy. He felt a twinge of guilt that he was about to try his best to make sure the goal stood. In truth, it really didn't look like the ball *had* completely crossed the line.

Then he remembered the 2010 Frank Lampard no-goal, and his moment of madness passed. He was doing this for his country. For England. And for Frank.

The referee was now hurrying towards him. Heart pounding in his chest, Rory strode forward onto the pitch to meet him.

The referee fixed him with an urgent, enquiring look and said something in Swiss. From his expression and body language, it was clearly along the lines of 'What did *you* think?'.

Rory went for it.

'Da! Da! Goalsky!' He concentrated hard on doing his best (not great) Russian accent. 'Da!

Goalsky!' He threw in some very earnest nodding and finger-wagging. 'Nyet problemov! Goalsky! Da! Da!'

It worked. The referee seemed to get the vital message loud and clear. He showed no sign of suspecting that his linesman was an impostor – let alone a non-Russian speaking twenty-first century time traveller disguised by an alien shape-changing device. He simply nodded back at Rory, then raised an arm and gave a shrill blast on his whistle. The goal had been awarded.

As the referee turned and jogged back towards the centre spot, Rory felt a flood of relief. He was only vaguely aware of the several West German players who came rushing up seconds later to confront him. He knew as little German as he did Russian, but he was pretty sure from the players' angry expressions that they weren't saying "thank you".

He didn't care. He'd done it. It was 3-2 to England, like it had always been meant to be.

The match was quickly restarted from the centre-spot. As Rory watched the two teams continue to fight it out, he could clearly see how much the Hurst goal had lifted the spirits of the English players. They looked revitalised and resolute.

Despite his aching stomach and throbbing head, Rory was glad he'd stepped into the missing linesman's shoes. Watching the England players pass the ball about confidently, he was more convinced than ever that the Bakhramov decision was a crucial turning point in the match. Now, surely, England ought to be safely on their way to their famous victory.

Nevertheless, as the match moved into the second period of extra time, Rory awaited the final whistle as anxiously as the many millions of his countrymen watching with him.

Come on, England…

CHAPTER 17
A SHOCKING ENCOUNTER

Amy took the steps down to the platform three at a time. She had left the indignant ticket attendant in the capable hands of PC Sanderson. The constable was even now calmly explaining to the man why Amy had just jumped the barrier. As she sprinted away, Amy had heard him speaking earnestly of "police business" and "national security".

She bounded down the last few steps and dashed onto the platform. Although Wembley Park station was part of the London Underground network, it was not *actually* underground. The train tracks here ran in the open air, as they did in many outer parts of the city.

A northbound Metropolitan Line train was just pulling out of the nearest platform. Perfect. That should mean she had a little time before the next train was due.

Amy hurried to the platform's edge and quickly lowered herself down onto the track. Thankfully, the station was deserted. There were no well-meaning bystanders to attempt to stop her. Most Londoners were following the big match, no doubt – blissfully unaware that the final whistle might signal the end of London life as they knew it.

Amy took a good look at the track, wondering where best to make the connection. There were three rails, as on all Underground tracks. The outer two were for the carriage wheels to run on. The middle rail carried the electricity that powered the trains – enough electricity to kill her, Amy knew, if she accidentally touched the rail.

She turned to lay one of the two crocodile-clip connectors on the platform edge. Holding the other, she stepped over the near-side rail, then carefully crouched down over the central electrified one.

Gotta get this right... thought Amy anxiously. If she fastened the connector in the wrong place, it would simply be knocked off by the next train. That wouldn't do.

But if I clip it on from underneath...

Amy squeezed the insulated handles of the connector together, and very gingerly clamped its jaws to the underside of the electrified rail. Her hand was shaking a little. But not enough, thankfully, to make contact with the rail.

She twisted the red handle of the connector, as the Doctor had told her, to activate it. Then she carefully released her grip. The connector stayed clamped in place, tucked out of the way of any passing wheels, and more or less out of sight. So far so good.

Amy had been so intent on avoiding electrocution that she had failed to notice that the two outer rails were giving off a faint whistling hum. She heard it now. The hum was quickly growing louder.

There was a train coming.

Amy fought against her fatal instinct to freeze with fear. Instead, she sprang back over the near-side rail and hauled herself up over the platform's edge. As she rolled away from it, a blast of air and noise rushed over her. A silvery blur rattled past – another A-Stock Metropolitan Line train pulling into the station.

As the train gradually slowed, Amy got to her feet and brushed herself down. She felt more than a little shaky. She had narrowly missed plenty of trains before. But she had never had one narrowly miss her.

She bent down to pick up the second connector. According to the Doctor, twisting this one's red handle would channel a flow of current from the electrical source to which its partner was attached. He had seemed confident that this 'cordless extension lead' of his could carry the Tube track's kilovolt supply.

The newly-arrived train drew to a halt. As it did so, Amy heard a clattering noise from the far end of the platform. It sounded very familiar. The eerie feeling that she wasn't alone came over her once more.

The train doors sliced open. Two passengers stepped out from the door nearest Amy. A couple more disembarked from a carriage further along the train. Not many people were getting off. Just the four.

But that was enough.

Amy stared hard at the spot where she had heard the clattering a moment ago. A distinct area of seemingly empty space, near the end of the platform, had begun flickering unnaturally. Amy had little difficulty recognising its shape and size.

She had been right all along. One of the adult Vispics *had* followed her from the stadium. It had used its sophisticated camouflage to stay hidden. But now, in trying to conceal itself from more than one person – the passengers that had just joined Amy on the platform – the creature had become partially visible.

Not for long. The handful of passengers were already heading up the steps towards the station's exit. To her horror, Amy watched the flickering patch of air become still. The Vispic was once more focussing on her alone.

The clattering noise came again. This time it grew rapidly nearer. Amy backed away helplessly, sensing that the camouflaged creature was attacking.

At the last moment, a desperate idea sprang into her mind. She clutched the connector in both hands, thrust it out at arm's length, and twisted the red handle.

The Doctor had warned Amy about the danger of activating the current. He had told her that she was not, on any account, to twist both red handles. A thousand volts could kill her stone dead.

Or save her skin.

The creature slammed into Amy just as she activated the connector. It got the shock of its life. As Amy sprawled backwards onto the platform, she kept firm hold of the connector's handles. A crackling web of white, lightning-like electricity leapt from the jaws of the connector and danced wildly around the outer surface of the Vispic's body.

The powerful jolt stunned the alien creature. It became fully visible. With an unearthly screech, it recoiled from Amy's improvised weapon. It collapsed clumsily on its side on the platform, where it lay twitching, ribbons of white energy still skittering across its grotesque body.

Amy twisted back the connector handle and hurriedly scrambled to her feet. She stared wide-eyed at the Vispic. It looked like the largest of the three that she and the Doctor had encountered under the South Stand. She wondered, for a moment, if she had killed it. But even as she looked, the creature began to stir. The electric shock had stunned it – that was all.

Amy didn't hang around to watch it recover fully. She turned, and sprinted for the stairs. She bounded up them towards the station exit, pulse racing. Only at the top did she glance back over her shoulder.

The Vispic had vanished.

Amy put her head down, and ran for her life.

Outside the Wembley Park station entrance, PC Sanderson was waiting anxiously on his patrol bike.

Agent Beckham – the red-haired whirlwind who had come ripping into his life and turned it upside down – had told him to be ready to make a hasty departure. She had spent the journey to the station with her arms wrapped tightly round him, yelling instructions in his ear over the growl of the Thunderbird's powerful engine. Once she'd done what she had to do at the Tube station, she'd explained, she needed him to get her to the Empire Stadium as fast as possible.

Sanderson smiled to himself. *Looks like I'm going to Wembley after all,* he thought.

To his surprise, he realised that he hadn't given the big match a thought for the last fifteen minutes or so. It had been driven from his mind by the fascinating stranger from Special Branch, with her sci-fi technology, and her talk of alien invaders.

And here she came now.

Sanderson saw her burst from the entrance of the Underground station. She was running like the devil himself was after her, and clutching just one of those giant crocodile clips she had brought with them.

At the sight of him, she gave a wild yell.

'Start your engine!'

Sanderson did as he was told. He stamped down on the Thunderbird's kick-starter, and the bike's engine roared into life. He shuffled forward on its leather saddle, to make sure there was room for his pillion passenger.

But before she could reach him, Agent Beckham stumbled and fell flat on her face. She had gone down as though something had caught her by the leg.

But there's nothing there...

Sanderson saw her twist onto her back. She thrust the connector she was clinging to fiercely upwards. A blaze of crackling electricity erupted from its tip. Sanderson was temporarily dazzled. But as the sparks faded, what he saw made his heart falter.

Oh... my...

Any remaining doubts about the young woman's alien-invasion story vanished from Sanderson's mind. A huge, hideous creature was lying on the pavement beside her. It had appeared out of nowhere. It was twitching horribly, its gross body sparking and smoking from the electric shock it had just sustained. But Sanderson could see that it was still undeniably alive.

He gunned the Thunderbird's engine. As its rear wheel span, squealing, on the tarmac, he threw the bike's back end around. The motorcycle mounted the pavement, and raced towards where Agent Beckham was now struggling to her feet. Sanderson sent it into another sweeping skid, so that its rear end came to a screeching halt right beside her.

'Jump on!'

As the young woman leapt astride the saddle behind him, Sanderson saw the alien thing begin to stir itself with more vigour. At close range, it was even more grotesque. And it was quickly recovering.

'Hold on tight!'

Agent Beckham didn't need telling twice. She wrapped her arms around Sanderson's waist, and clung on. The young police officer opened up the motorbike's throttle once more.

The Thunderbird roared across Bridge Road, out onto Olympic Way, and headed south, towards Wembley.

CHAPTER 18

THE TWIN TOWERS

Amy's burning worry now was that she wouldn't reach the Doctor in time. She had made the connection to the electrified Tube rail. She was still in possession of the second connector, which would allow the Doctor to feed the Underground's supply into his voltage-boosting device. But what if she and PC Sanderson couldn't find him fast enough once they reached the stadium?

Amy knew there could be only minutes left before the football match ended, and the Vispic larvae began to feast. Only minutes left to destroy the displacement anchor, and save London.

But finding the Doctor proved less of a problem than Amy had feared. Only moments after PC

Sanderson brought his patrol bike to a skidding halt outside the main stadium entrance, and Amy quickly dismounted, she heard a familiar yell.

'Ahoy there, Amelia Pond! Glad you could make it!'

Amy looked up. She wasn't sure whether to feel relieved or horrified by what she saw. It was good to have found the Doctor so quickly. But what *was* he doing up there?

A thin silver wire stretched all the way from the flagpole on top of one of the stadium's twin white towers to the flagpole on the other. Halfway along it, dangling by one hand, was the Doctor. The Vispic displacement anchor was clasped in his other hand.

There was an alarming distance from the wire to the stadium roof below. Amy seriously hoped he knew what he was doing.

'I've got the extension lead!' she yelled back. She held the connector high so that the Doctor could see it. 'It's all plugged in, courtesy of London Transport!'

'Splendid work, Pond! Who's your friend?'

PC Sanderson had now also dismounted. He was standing beside Amy, gawping at the Doctor's daredevil high-wire act. He turned to look at her, puzzled.

'Amelia Pond?' That wasn't the name she had given *him*.

'Er…' Amy looked awkward. 'Yeah. It's… um… another Special Branch codename.'

She hastily turned her attention back to the Doctor.

'This, Agent Lineker,' she yelled, 'is PC Sanderson. He got me back here in one piece!'

'Good man, Sanderson!' The Doctor now appeared to be attaching the displacement anchor to the midpoint of the wire with his free hand. A moment later, he let go of the slim filament. It stayed in place.

'Right! That's it! She's all set! We just need to connect up the juice!'

Amy and Sanderson watched anxiously as the Doctor began to make his way, hand over hand, along the wire, back towards the right-hand tower. He was almost halfway to the flagpole when he suddenly stopped.

'What's the matter, Doctor?' yelled Amy.

'Do me a favour, both of you!' he hollered back. 'Keep looking at that tower dome.'

Amy and Sanderson did as he asked. Both fixed their eyes on the dome.

It took Amy a few seconds to see it. One area of the white dome was flickering unnaturally.

'Thought so!' yelled the Doctor. Swinging precariously by one arm again, he quickly pulled out his sonic screwdriver. He aimed it at the right-hand tower dome. A thin, metre-long bolt of green light suddenly shot from its tip.

As the energy pulse struck it, the flickering shape that Amy had made out solidified into a hideous, multi-limbed body. The adult Vispic that was clinging to the dome became fully visible – almost highlighted, in fact, as its entire alien body turned bright orange.

'I've calculated a frequency that messes up their

skin-pigment control,' the Doctor shouted down. 'Fixes it temporarily in one tone. At least I can see what I'm dealing with!'

He twisted his arm to turn his dangling body through one hundred and eighty degrees.

'And unless I'm much mistaken…'

He took aim, and fired off another sonic pulse, in the direction of the other tower dome. A moment later, the hulking body of a second adult Vispic became clearly visible, crouching atop the dome. This time, its skin colour had been locked shocking pink all over.

The twin creatures lurking on the twin towers were the size of the smaller adult Vispics Amy and the Doctor had met earlier. These two had come after the Doctor – just as the larger adult had come after Amy. It looked likely that the Vispics had figured out that Amy and the Doctor were planning something, and were out to stop them.

The Doctor's situation didn't look good. He was now hanging from the wire between the two flagpoles, with a hungry Vispic lying in wait for him at each of its ends. He had been left with nowhere to go.

Amy saw the dangling Doctor look from one Vispic to the other, then down at her.

'Wish me luck, Pond!' he yelled down. 'Because as much as I'd *love* to hang around...'

Amy let out a shriek of horror as the Doctor let go of the wire, and fell.

'DOCTOR!'

The Doctor's body plummeted to the stadium roof, dropping out of Amy's field of vision. She stared at the point where he had vanished, waiting and hoping for a sign that he was okay.

Several seconds passed. Still nothing.

Then, suddenly, Amy saw the Doctor's wild-haired head poke out from over the edge of the roof. He was grinning playfully.

'Did you miss me?'

Amy, craning her neck, gave him an exasperated look. She saw his smile vanish at the sound of two heavy crashes. The Vispics had jumped down from their tower perches to join him on the stadium roof.

'No need to panic!' the Doctor yelled down. 'They'll be displaced as soon as we connect the power!' His right hand appeared over the edge of the roof. It was clutching a coil of electrical cable – the old-fashioned black-and-white fabric covered kind.

'I'm going to throw this down, Pond! Just clamp the connector to the end, and switch it on!'

'Is that going to take a thousand volts, Doctor?' From where Amy was standing, the cable didn't look particularly heavy-duty.

'I've tweaked the core!' yelled back the Doctor. 'It's super-conductive now. It'll be fine. Ready?'

Before Amy could reply, there was an anxious shout from PC Sanderson.

'Agent Beckham!'

Amy turned to see what the problem was.

The third adult Vispic – the largest one – was clattering towards them along Olympic Way. It looked more bizarre than ever. Its camouflage seemed to be only partly working. Bits of its body were clearly visible, while other parts still matched themselves to their background, giving the overall impression of a grotesque, moth-eaten monster.

Amy guessed that the double shocks she had given the Vispic back at the Tube station had taken their toll on the creature's camouflage. Or maybe it was just mad enough not to care whether they could see it.

Either way, it was still perfectly capable of making a meal of her and Sanderson. They needed to make that connection, fast.

Amy turned back to look up at the Doctor on the rooftop.

'Ready, Doctor! Lob it down!'

The Doctor let the cable drop. It uncoiled down the stadium wall as it fell. Amy put her arms out to catch its free end.

But it didn't reach her. Not even nearly. Even as its full length dangled down the face of the wall, its end hung a good seven or eight metres from the ground.

The cable was too short.

CHAPTER 19
THE DYING SECONDS

If the final whistle didn't come soon, Rory was going to keel over. He wasn't sure which was more unbearable – the effect of the shimmer on his poor, aching body, or the atmosphere of raw nervous tension that now filled the Empire Stadium.

West Germany had clearly decided that they had nothing to lose. There were only a few minutes of the second period of extra time left to play, and they were still a goal down. They were throwing everyone forward, in a last-ditch attempt to save the match.

The English fans in the crowd were watching the dying seconds in a frenzy of nervous anticipation. Victory had already been snatched from the English once, only half an hour earlier. They wouldn't dare believe this match was won until it was over.

Rory knew that he *shouldn't* be sharing their anxiety. After all, *he* knew how the result would turn out. Or, at least, how it was *meant* to turn out. But somehow, his nerves were on a knife-edge, too. After all, it would only take one moment of German skill to change the scoreline to 3-3.

There was nothing more *he* could do. He had done his bit. Or, to be more accurate, he had done Bakhramov's bit. Surely history *must* be back on track.

He watched anxiously as the West German players pressed forward again. There was a tremendous roar from the crowd as Ray Wilson bravely slid in to steal the ball. The England fans were cheering every tackle now.

Rory checked his watch yet again. They were into injury time. England just had to keep hold of the ball…

But moments later, the West Germans had won possession once more. Beckenbauer began a dangerous, weaving run into the English half.

'Come on!' muttered Rory to himself. 'Blow, ref, blow!'

Outside the stadium, the situation was equally tense.

As soon as it had become obvious that the Doctor's cable was not going to reach her, Amy had resolved to find a way to reach *it*.

Climbing was not her greatest strength at the best of times. Climbing the sheer face of a large building, which offered few handholds or footholds, was proving a real challenge. A very painful, very scary challenge.

She had now made it nearly six metres up the stadium's wall. She was clinging on for dear life, with one hand and both feet somehow maintaining their purchase on the slightest of holds, while she felt about desperately above her for another ridge or ledge by which to pull herself up. She had the crocodile-clip connector clamped firmly between her teeth.

The exposed end of the cable dangled tantalisingly close overhead. It was only a metre or so out of her reach.

Amy could feel the strength ebbing from her arms. The drop to the concrete below made her feel light-headed. She felt sure she would lose her grip at any moment.

But she *had* to keep going. All she had to do was get to the cable, and make the connection. Just a few more centimetres…

On the ground below Amy, PC Sanderson was showing similar bravery in the face of danger. By now, the largest of the adult Vispics – the one that Amy had fought off at the Tube station – would have overcome both of them, were it not for the policeman's desperate actions.

As the Vispic came scuttling into the stadium's forecourt from Olympic Way, Sanderson had leapt back onto his faithful Thunderbird, and kick-started the bike's powerful engine. With little thought for his own safety, he had driven the bike straight at the charging Vispic. He was determined to keep the alien beast from harming Amy, at all costs.

His headlong motorcycle charge had worked. The Vispic was forced to throw itself to one side to avoid a collision. It came to a halt, then began to scuttle first one way, then the other, weighing up its reckless opponent.

The two were now engaged in a one-on-one stand-off, like the world's most bizarre bullfight. Man-and-machine against alien monster.

Meanwhile, up on the stadium's roof, the Doctor was being kept fully occupied by the other adult Vispics. They were having their own pitched battle. It was playing out between the stadium's gleaming twin towers. The two smaller Vispics were circling the Doctor menacingly, while he brandished his sonic screwdriver like a sword.

It didn't look like a fight the Doctor could win. But so far, at least, he had managed to evade each sudden, vicious attack – thanks to some well-timed dodging, and the odd blast of stinging sonic energy.

Down on the ground, the Vispic began its next charge. Sanderson boldly urged the Thunderbird forward to meet it head on.

But this time, the alien creature got the better of him. It dipped its ugly hammerhead at the last moment, then threw it back, flipping the front wheel of the police bike into the air. Sanderson lost control of it completely. He was thrown from the Thunderbird's saddle. His body hit the forecourt, skidded across it a considerable distance, then lay still. His motorcycle screeched to a standstill on its side, some way away.

The Vispic had no further interest in Sanderson for now. It clearly understood what Amy was attempting to do – and was intent only on stopping her. It scuttled to the base of the wall she was clinging to, and began to climb.

To Amy's great dismay, it seemed Vispic leeches made better climbers than girls from Leadworth. Only moments later, she felt an alien claw clutch at her trailing leg. She risked losing her grip by kicking down hard with one foot. She landed a solid blow on the Vispic's head, and a moment or two later had the satisfaction of hearing the creature hit the ground below, with a clatter.

Amy frantically scrabbled to regain her foothold, then peered down anxiously.

The Vispic was already beginning to climb the wall again.

Bobby Moore, the England captain, won the ball deep in his own half. He looked up, and in a typically inspired moment, spotted the perfect pass to play. The desperate West Germans had pushed up so far, they had left themselves wide open to a fast counter-attack. Moore picked out Geoff Hurst in space on the left wing, and sent a gloriously well-judged ball into his team mate's path.

From the touchline, Rory watched Hurst collect Moore's pass and begin streaking upfield with the ball. As he did so, all sense of anxiety lifted from him. Once again, Rory recognised this moment. He had re-lived it on YouTube countless times. It never lost its ability to fascinate and thrill him. What was about to happen, Rory knew, was the greatest moment in English football history.

'Go on, Geoff! GO ON!'

Rory cheered wildly as the England centre-forward ran past him, the ball at his feet. He didn't care any more that he was supposed to be Russian, or Azerbaijani, or whatever. Nor did he care that right at that moment, he had the most terrible stomach ache of his entire life.

All he cared about was what was about to happen.

After two hours of full-on football, Hurst somehow found the energy to sprint the entire length of the pitch. He took the ball past the final German outfield player. As he bore down on the German goal from the left wing, he drilled a powerful left-footed, long-range shot towards the top near corner of the net...

Amy, with one final heroic heave, pulled herself up to within reach of the dangling cable. She let go of the wall with her right hand, risking a deadly fall, and pulled the connector from her mouth. She stretched the fingers of her right hand to their limit to grasp both its handles, and squeezed them together.

Something cold and sharp scraped against the back of her right leg.

She desperately raised the connector until its jaws were around the exposed cable end, clamped it on, and gave the red handle a firm twist.

One thousand volts of electricity instantly surged along the cable. It flowed into the complex inverter-transformer circuit that the Doctor had ingeniously engineered from Wembley's vast aluminium roof structure. The voltage was boosted a hundred-fold, before the pulse finally shot up the flagpole of the left-hand stadium tower, and along the wire that connected it to the other pole.

The displacement anchor, secured at the midpoint of the wire, glowed brilliantly, blindingly white for an instant. Then it exploded into a million tiny pieces, like a puff of glittering powder.

All three adult Vispics vanished in the blink of an eye. Amy, the Doctor and PC Sanderson, who had now struggled back to his feet, found themselves alone.

And all along the north-west branch of the Metropolitan Line, bewildered London Transport employees wondered why the Tube trains they were driving had just ground to a halt.

Amy wasn't out of danger yet. The last drop of strength in her left-hand fingertips was draining away fast. She couldn't hold on much longer. With one last exertion, she twisted back the red connector handle to kill the power. Then she scrabbled at the wall hopelessly with her right hand. But there was nothing to grip.

Her left foot slipped, and she fell.

A split second later, she found herself dangling in thin air – but *not* falling through it. Something was clinging to her right wrist. A hand.

'Gotcha!'

Amy looked up into the anxious face of the Doctor. Much of it was covered by his drooping hair, which had flopped forward, due to the fact that he was hanging almost upside down. Somehow, he had managed to drop from the stadium roof, down the power cable, in time to catch her.

'Nice work, Agent Beckham!'

Despite the effort he was clearly putting into keeping hold of her, the Doctor forced a smile.

'Never doubted for a moment that you had things under control!'

Amy looked up at him, her pale face paler than ever.

'Did we do it, Doctor?' she asked. 'Are they gone? Do you think it's all over?'

At that moment, a deafening roar rose from inside the stadium – the roar of tens of thousands of rejoicing spectators. Hurst had scored his third goal. The match was over. England had beaten West Germany, four goals to two.

And under the South Stand, not a single luck-sucking larva remained to feast on the elation of the euphoric English fans.

As the Doctor replied to Amy, his grin broadened.

'It is now!'

EPILOGUE

The Doctor, Amy and Rory turned off Olympic Way and strolled eastward along the Fulton Road.

The city streets were very different from the last time Amy had made this journey, alone. The pavements were packed with celebrating England supporters. Some had spilled from the stadium itself. Others were Londoners who had left their homes to join the party. They were chanting, singing, waving their Union Jacks, or simply clinging to one another in sheer delight.

As the three friends crossed the street, they had to hurry out of the path of a human snake of whooping revellers, dancing the conga – *"Dada-*

da-da-da-da… PAH!" – along the centre of the road.

Despite the party atmosphere, Amy felt a little weary to be making this particular trek again.

'I still don't see why you couldn't let Bill give me a lift,' she grumbled. She had enjoyed riding pillion on the young police officer's patrol bike. It would have been even pleasanter without a pursuing alien.

'He has better things to do, Pond,' said the Doctor. 'Good man, that Sanderson. I thought we could trust him to tidy up a few loose ends.'

In fact, the Doctor – in his role as Agent Lineker – had assigned the helpful constable a number of important tasks before they parted company back at the stadium. Sanderson was to check on the condition of the unconscious Bakhramov, and when the linesman revived, order him not to say a word about his peculiar experience. He was also to recover the body of the Vispics' victim – the man they had found in the changing room – and ensure that his death was put down to natural causes, so as to prevent unnecessary alarm. Finally, he was to keep this entire Code Thirteen affair secret – for reasons of National Security.

The Doctor had made it very clear that he and Agent Beckham, and indeed the entire population of London, owed PC Sanderson a great debt of thanks. Special Branch would watch his career with interest.

'Aww! It's shut!' complained Rory. They were approaching Syd Marlin's news-stand once again, where the Doctor had bought his paper earlier. 'I was gonna get a few more of those player stickers...'

'Ooh – wait a second!' The Doctor came to a halt, and began rooting about in his pockets. He pulled out several coins. Although the news-stand was closed, there was a narrow gap under its shutters. The Doctor poked several of the larger coins through this gap.

'Just a few shillings, or florins, or groats, or whatever they are – in case I *didn't* pay that chap enough...'

They set off along the pavement again. A group

of happy fans hailed them from the other side of the road. The young men whirled their football rattles. Over the loud *tatta-tatta-tatta* sound, they began a rousing chorus of "Rule Britannia".

Rory was carrying a rattle of his own. He had told Amy, when they had eventually managed to regroup after the match, that he had found it, and decided to keep hold of it as a souvenir.

Rory was in particularly high spirits. England had just become world champions, after all. And it was a huge relief to have removed the shimmer at last. Rory couldn't describe how good it was to feel – and look – like himself again. No more dodgy tummy and daft tash.

His only regret was that neither Amy nor the Doctor had seen his moment of glory. They didn't seem to have caught *any* of the match, in fact. When Rory had asked Amy why not, she had just snapped that they had been "a little bit busy".

Rory saluted the singing fans with an enthusiastic whirl of his own wooden rattle. He saw Amy wince at the noise it made.

'What?' Rory gave her a hurt look. 'Aw, come on, Amy! I just single-handedly rescued England's World Cup win. I deserve *something* to remember it by, don't I?'

Amy didn't answer. Instead, she changed the subject.

'Speaking of "remembering" – you two haven't forgotten our deal, right?' She gave both Rory and the Doctor a steely look. 'About where we're taking the TARDIS next? I only agreed to come here on the condition that we go straight on to see the final when *Scotland* win, remember?'

'Yes, Pond,' said the Doctor. 'We recall.'

'Good. So long as that's understood, boys.'

'You're absolutely sure the Scots *do* win it sometime, Doctor?' Rory clearly found this hard to swallow. 'I mean, the *actual* World Cup?'

Amy came to an abrupt halt. She confronted Rory, hands on hips.

'And why shouldn't they?'

There was danger in Amy's fiery glare. Rory opened his mouth to reply. But the Doctor cut in, before things turned nasty.

'I guarantee, Rory, that Scotland are future world champions,' he said quickly. 'As you will both duly see for yourselves.'

Amy gave Rory a fierce "so there" look, then strode off along the pavement again.

'Though we are talking about the very, *very* far-off, future-y future,' the Doctor added, in a whispered aside to Rory. Rory grinned at him. They set off after Amy.

'Anyway, another football outing is cool by me,' said Rory, as they caught up with her. 'But this time I'm *not* getting involved. Strictly spectating. *Come… on… you… blues!*'

As he practised his supporter's chant, he gave his wooden rattle another enthusiastic whirl. *Tatta-tatta-tatta!*

Without warning, Amy snatched the rattle from Rory's grasp. Before he could stop her, she stepped off the pavement, held it over a storm drain, and let it drop. The rattle vanished down a gap in the drain's grating.

'Amy!' Rory was devastated. 'What did you do *that* for?'

Amy simply brushed off her hands theatrically.

Once again, the Doctor stepped in as peacekeeper.

'Never mind, Rory,' he said briskly. 'Between you and me, I've got an idea for a *much* better World Cup memento. Less noisy, too.'

Rory continued to sulk.

'It would, however, involve us making a *very* brief stop-off on the way to the Scotland final,' the Doctor told Amy. 'How do you feel about a quick detour to Rio de Janeiro?'

'Brazil?' Amy frowned. 'What for?'

'The headquarters of the Brazilian Football Confederation to be precise,' the Doctor continued, evading Amy's question. 'December 19th, 1983. Around midnight, shall we say?'

Now Rory couldn't help being intrigued.

'I know that date,' he said. 'That's when the Jules Rimet Trophy gets stolen for the second time.' His eyes widened. 'You don't mean…? What, that *we* could...?'

The Doctor grinned mischievously. 'Better than petty thieves having it, don't you think?'

Rory beamed from ear to ear. The World Cup itself. As a souvenir. Wicked.

Amy reached a junction and turned left, leading the others round the corner. They were back on Albion Way, where they had first arrived. There were the two dark blue police call boxes, side by side.

Amy hesitated for a moment.

'*There* you are, old girl!' The Doctor strode eagerly towards the left-hand box. Rory and Amy followed. The three of them halted in front of the TARDIS. The Doctor surveyed his faithful craft with an affectionate gaze.

'There's no mistaking the real McCain, eh, you two?'

'It's "*McCoy*", Doctor,' said Rory.

His words fell on deaf ears.

'Still stands out from the crowd, doesn't she?' the Doctor went on proudly.

'Absolutely,' agreed Amy. She looked a little shifty. 'Oh yeah. Unique.'

A sudden burst of raucous singing caused the three friends to look back towards Fulton Road. They watched another conga line of jubilant England fans dance their way across the end of the street.

'They certainly do love their football, the English, don't they?' said the Doctor. 'I can remember them going *just* as crazy next time they win it.'

He smiled, then turned his attention back to the TARDIS's doors.

It took Rory's brain a moment to register what the Doctor had just said.

'*Next* time?' He looked puzzled. Then an expression of pure elation slowly spread across his face. Of all the thousands of football facts stashed in Rory's head, not one was as exciting as this revelation.

'So – England *do* win the World Cup again? Yesss!' He did a little victory spin on one heel. 'I *knew* we could! When?'

But the Doctor and Amy were no longer beside him. They had already disappeared into the TARDIS.

'Doctor? *When*?!'

Rory hurried after them, closing the door behind him.

THE END

DOCTOR WHO

THE WATER THIEF

JACQUELINE RAYNER

CHAPTER 1

BESIDE THE SEASIDE

'The thing about the seaside,' said Amy, shielding her eyes and gazing into the distance, 'is that it's beside the sea. That's where the name comes from.'

The pretty redhead directed a mock frown towards the TARDIS as she waved a hand at the surrounding sand. There was very definitely no sea in sight. 'This is not the seaside. This is the sea-not-side.'

The Doctor came out of his time machine. He was wearing his usual tweed jacket, despite the fierce sun beating down outside the TARDIS, and was carrying a bucket and spade. He totally ignored Amy's frown. 'Ah, summer holiday,' he said with a happy sigh, and crouching down began to shovel sand into the bucket. 'Might be a bit tricky when we come to the moat, but there should be no problem with sandcastles.'

The third member of the TARDIS crew exited the police box. This was Rory, Amy's husband. He was frowning too, although unlike his wife's mock-anger he just looked confused. 'Southend's changed since I was last here,' he said. 'Where's the pier?'

'That's because it's not Southend, it's a desert,' Amy told him. 'Probably the desert planet of Sando or something.'

'Don't be silly,' said the Doctor, sniffing the air. 'Definitely Earth. It has a very distinctive scent, Earth. Sort of marshmallows and hope.' He upended his bucket and watched in dismay as the sand collapsed in a heap. 'Oh.'

'You need wet sand to make sandcastles,' Rory pointed out.

'I knew that,' said the Doctor. He bounced to his feet, leaving the bucket and spade lying forlornly behind him. 'Right, time to explore. Amy, to the wardrobe! You'll get sunstroke wandering around a desert like that, what were you thinking?'

'I was thinking I was going to the seaside,' muttered bikini-clad Amy.

'– and Rory, there are two long white things sticking out the bottom of your trousers, that can't be right.'

'I'm wearing shorts, they're my legs,' said Rory wearily. 'I just don't tan easily, that's all.'

'Well, wait here a moment...' The Doctor vanished into the TARDIS, reappearing a few minutes later minus his jacket but carrying a large bundle of cloth. Soon the three time travellers were dressed in long, flowing white robes with white scarves wrapped around their heads.

'Well, look at you, Lawrence of Arabia!' said Amy admiringly. Rory grinned.

The Doctor handed out water bottles. 'Can't be too careful,' he said.

'But where are we going?' asked Rory. 'We can't just walk out into the desert, that'd be silly.'

'I thought,' said the Doctor, spinning on the

spot and pointing behind the TARDIS, 'that we'd have a look at that town over there.'

Amy and Rory followed his pointing finger. Sure enough, there was some sort of settlement in the distance.

'Oh,' said Rory. 'Right.'

And they set off.

'Hang on, what's that?' said Rory after they'd been walking for a little while.

The Doctor peered ahead. 'Aha!' he said. 'Interesting. Tents.'

'Campsite? Music festival? Nomads?' Amy asked.

The Doctor grinned. 'Archaeological excavation! Come on!'

They picked up speed. As they got closer, they could make out a number of dark-skinned men hacking at the sand with picks. Closer still, and a couple of paler-skinned men in light-coloured suits could be spotted too, walking here and there between the trenches. 'Oh, just look at those moustaches!' Amy whispered to Rory. 'Talk about having a gerbil sellotaped under your nose...'

One of the diggers noticed them approach and called out to his fellows. The two suited men looked up and started to stride across the sands towards them. The Doctor waved cheerily.

Surprise appeared on the men's faces as they reached the Doctor's party. 'You're English!' one said.

'Scottish...' murmured Amy.

'We thought from the clothes –' The man gestured at the white robes.

'Oh, we like to be comfy,' said the Doctor, grinning. 'Anyway, robes are cool. Literally. Keep out the heat, you know.'

The second man gave a short bow. 'You must forgive our rudeness. We weren't expecting visitors, especially Western ones. You're very welcome here.'

'Where is here?' asked Rory. 'We, er, got a bit lost.'

The first man pointed over his shoulder at the huts beyond the dig site. 'That is the village of Behneseh – such as it is,' he told them. 'Once the third most important city in Egypt with temple, theatre and thousands of prosperous citizens, reduced over the centuries to just a few squalid huts.'

Rory nudged Amy and mouthed 'Egypt!' excitedly. She mouthed back 'squalid huts' with slightly less excitement.

'Would you care for some refreshment?' asked the second man. 'I see you have water bottles with you, but if you have walked far across the desert I'm sure you will be ready for something more. A cup of tea, perhaps?'

'Lovely,' said the Doctor. 'Lead the way!'

They walked through the excavations, watched with interest by the diggers. Amy pulled Rory to one side. 'When d'you reckon we are – early twentieth century?'

'About then,' Rory agreed. 'Or Victorian maybe? That's when everyone in Britain went mad for Egyptian stuff, I think. Tutankhamun and all that sort of thing.'

'Tutankhamun!' Amy laughed. 'That's what Egypt should be about! Pharaohs! Pyramids!

Treasure! Baths of asses' milk! But we end up with no seaside holiday and squalid huts instead. Boring!'

Rory shook his head. 'I've seen the films. There're bound to be booby traps and ancient curses and walking mummies. Come on, this is the Doctor we're talking about. When has he ever taken us anywhere boring?'

Amy conceded the point. 'Excuse me,' she said to the two men, who turned to her politely. 'Can I ask what you're digging for here? Is it an ancient tomb?'

'Golden treasure?' suggested Rory.

'Cursed relics?' said Amy.

The men chuckled. 'Oh, something much more exciting than that!' said the first.

'Wow.' Amy was impressed.

'Yes,' said the second man. 'Papers!'

Amy waited for the exciting bit, but the man had finished speaking. 'Papers?' she said after a moment.

'Well, mostly papyri, a few parchments; we use the term merely for convenience.'

The Doctor jumped in. 'You see, Amy, for anyone who doesn't have a time machine, which is of course everybody, it's hard to discover what life was really like in the ancient world. Only really important documents tend to survive, those carved on stone for example. Historians might know a bit about important laws or great kings, but not a lot about, oooh, building regulations or the price of fish.'

'Yawn,' whispered Amy under her breath.

'That's right,' agreed the first man, luckily not seeming to have heard Amy's comment. 'But this is the most astonishing find. It will revolutionise our views of the ancient world!'

His friend nodded. 'The circumstances are unique. This,' – he gestured to the mound that the workers were still attacking with picks – 'was one of the many rubbish dumps for the city. Over the years the people threw away thousands upon thousands of documents, and the sand piled up over them. There is no rain here, so they lay preserved forever, safe and dry. Ready for us to find.'

Amy nudged Rory again. 'Squalid huts and rubbish dumps!' she whispered. 'The Doctor is really spoiling us!'

They were led down into a dip, sand giving way to dried mud. 'This was once a branch of the Nile river itself, a stretch of water known as Bahr Yussuf, but it is dry now. The servants have to walk some way to fetch water. But we have enough left for today to make tea.'

They climbed up the other side of the dip – it was clear, now it had been pointed out, that it was a dry river bed – and walked up a scrubby, dusty path to the village proper. A largish tent, a bit like a marquee, had been put up in the middle of the settlement, and it was into this tent they went. 'The cookhouse,' one of the archaeologists explained, as he lit a spirit stove and fetched a kettle to put on it. 'No open flames are allowed near the papyri.'

'Very sensible, Mr Grenfell,' said the Doctor. 'Or is Mr Hunt?'

'I am Grenfell, yes. You know us, sir?'

'Oh yes. Now I know what this place is and what

you're doing here – well, your reputations preceded you. Excellent work you're doing, gentlemen, excellent work. But where are my manners? Let me introduce Mr and Mrs Amy Pond –'

'Rory,' muttered Rory. 'Rory Williams. But I am Mr – I mean, she is Mrs – well, we are married.'

'– and I'm the Doctor. So now we all know each other, and tea may be drunk.'

The tea was not to Amy's taste, being sweet and black with tea leaves floating in it, but it was very welcome. The sun was beginning to sink in the sky now, and the earlier warmth was disappearing with it. She shivered.

The other man – Hunt – noticed her shaking. 'I hope we may offer you accommodation,' he said. 'It's very cold out in the desert at night. And of course, in the dark it's much harder to avoid the snakes and scorpions.'

'Snakes and scorpions!' echoed Amy, her voice rising. She gave the Doctor a hard stare. 'I don't believe either snakes or scorpions were in the brochure.'

'It's all right, Amy,' Rory put in. 'They'd be more scared of you than you are of them.'

'Idiot, that's what people say about spiders! Not snakes and scorpions!'

'Oh, there are spiders in the desert too,' said Grenfell helpfully. 'About as big as your hand, but not really that poisonous.'

'Yes, thank you, we would like to stay here tonight,' Amy told him before the Doctor or Rory could speak. 'Anything non-deserty will do.'

'Wouldn't mind a look at those papyri first, though,' said the Doctor. 'Before the light goes. If that's all right?'

'Of course,' said Hunt.

'Be still my beating heart,' Amy muttered.

'Come on, you might be surprised,' Rory whispered back.

But Rory didn't suspect just how big a surprise was in store for them...

CHAPTER 2

BISCUIT TIN OF SURPRISES

The two archaeologists seemed delighted at the Doctor's interest in their discoveries, and led the travellers out of the tent and to a mud-brick hut a little way away. There were two camp beds on the floor, but most of the space was taken up with metal boxes. 'Here we sort our day's finds before having them shipped back to Oxford,' Hunt said, taking a box from a shelf and opening it. 'Our plan is to spend half the year here in Egypt, working at the dig, and the other half translating and cataloguing our discoveries back home.'

He took a scrap of ancient-looking papyrus out of the metal box – an old biscuit tin – and laid it out carefully on a trestle table. The visitors peered at it. '"Whom the gods love die young",' Amy read out loud. 'Well, that's us – we've died, what, three times between us so far, Rory?'

She'd said the last bit under her breath, but when she saw the amazed looks on the faces of Grenfell and Hunt, she assumed they must have heard her. After all, what was an everyday sort of thing for people who travelled in time and space sounded like madness to most people! But she soon realised it was actually her first few words that had surprised them.

'My word, a young lady who can read Greek!' exclaimed Hunt. 'How wonderful! And how extraordinary!'

'Pray tell where you were taught this skill,' said Grenfell, just as amazed. 'A girls' school that teaches Greek, indeed!'

'For a start,' began Amy indignantly, but the Doctor jumped in quickly.

'Very progressive parents, home educated, actually we can all read it,' he said before Amy could continue. 'A trio of wandering classical Greek scholars, that's us. Or rather, linguists in general. Greek, Latin, Hebrew, Old High Gallifreyan...' He plucked another document from the tin and began to read it out loud. '"Dear Mum, hope you are well, the weather here continues hot" – hmm, Ancient Egyptian postcard, interesting. Well, not interesting exactly, but...' He trailed off as Hunt and Grenfell turned their astonished stares to him.

'The speed of your translation!' Hunt cried. 'Incredible.'

'Well, I don't like to boast...' the Doctor said modestly. He reached forward to pick up another paper. 'Ooh, now, this is interesting. The colour. Not come across papyri like this before, wonder what it means?'

'Pretty,' commented Amy, peering over his shoulder.

'Ah yes, that tinge of purple – very unusual,' said Grenfell. 'Of course, purple was the colour of royalty throughout much of the ancient world, we wondered if perhaps a touch of dye was added during the process of turning the plant into paper for important documents. This, as you can see, is the funeral spells – the Book of the Dead – for an important man.'

'Interesting,' said the Doctor. 'Of course, parchments dyed purple were found in the Roman and Byzantine empires, but were for use only by emperors, and usually had gold or silver lettering. And they were a much deeper, reddy colour, rather than this lilac tint. Now that's interesting...' He had unrolled the scroll a little further and was peering at the paper with a frown on his face.

Hunt and Grenfell were beaming at him now. 'A true scholar of the ancient world!' said Hunt. 'What a lucky day it was for us when you came this way, Doctor. All of you! This young lady here,' – he turned to Amy – 'that she was a scholar of such accomplishment I never guessed when first I spied her...'

Rory had been peering dreamily into the distance, not paying much attention to what was going on. But he heard Hunt's last words. 'Spider!' he yelled suddenly, and dived forward. 'Don't worry, Amy, I'll protect you!'

Amy swung round as Rory tried to get in front of her. He tripped over her feet, and as husband and wife ended up in a heap on the floor, the remains of Rory's cup of tea flew through the air, splashing on to the papyrus in the Doctor's hand.

'Oh no, no!' Rory said, as the Doctor tried unsuccessfully to shake it dry.

Hunt and Grenfell were models of courtesy. Grenfell helped Amy to her feet while Hunt assured Rory that no damage had been done, even though that was obviously untrue.

'It's still readable,' said the Doctor. He sighed. 'Untouched by moisture for two thousand years, then along comes Rory. It's not for nothing that we call him Mr Pond – gettit? Water – pond?'

'I'm married to Amy, and her name's Pond, so they call me Mr Pond even though it's not my name,' Rory explained again. 'And I'm really, really sorry about the papyrus...'

'Don't mention it, please,' Hunt insisted. 'The Doctor's right, the ink has not run and once it's dried out it will be fine. For now, let us work out where you will sleep tonight, and then I hope you will join us for the evening meal.'

The workers were returning from the dig by the time two storage tents had been emptied to make room for the three visitors. A savoury smell was coming from the cookhouse tent, and the men – over a hundred of them, by Amy's reckoning – filed in to collect a dish of food each. Amy, Rory and the Doctor joined the queue, then sat down with Grenfell and Hunt to eat. Rory kept on apologising about the ruined papyrus.

'I won't hear another word,' Hunt told him. 'My plan is to leave it in the cookhouse as that's the warmest place here at night-time, then we'll see what it looks like in the morning. It'll be perfectly safe, our cook, Gahiji, sleeps there.'

'Besides,' added Grenfell, 'the help that the three of you can give us in our translation work more than makes up for your unfortunate accident. Oh –' he looked embarrassed, 'I may be presuming too much.'

'Oh no, we'd be delighted to stay on and help,' said the Doctor. 'For a little while, anyway.'

The sun was very low now, and people started to drift away to their beds. The two tents, one for Amy and Rory and a separate one for the Doctor, were near the outskirts of the village, on the banks of what had once been the river.

Two minutes after they'd been left alone, a knock came on the door of Rory and Amy's tent – or at least something that they guessed was supposed to be a knock, although it was rather canvas-y. The Doctor undid the ties holding the doorflaps together and popped his head through the gap.

'Come on in, then, we're all decent,' Amy told him. 'You seem to know all about those archaeologists, are they famous or something? Ooh, is a terrible ancient curse about to be unleashed? We said, Rory, didn't we, that a terrible ancient curse was probably about to be unleashed. Is that how you know about them?'

'The reason I know about them,' said the Doctor, 'is because as should have become clear by now, this is a very significant archaeological discovery. 1896 to 1906, Grenfell and Hunt excavated here for ten years. OK, so they might call it Behneseh, but this is Oxyrhynchus, home of the most famous rubbish tips in the world! Well over half the ancient plays, poetry and so on known by your time were discovered here. And that's just the tip of the iceberg!'

'Ancient plays and poems that unleash a terrible curse when read?' Amy suggested hopefully.

'No,' said the Doctor firmly.

'Boring,' said Amy.

Rory changed the subject. 'Paypyrus, that's made from reeds, right?'

'From the pith of the papyrus plant,' the Doctor replied. 'Ooh, try saying that a few times fast. The pith of the papyrus plant, the pith of the papyrus plant, the pith –'

'Yes, thank you, we've got the idea,' said Amy,

trying to look stern and not laugh.

'So, er, are they going to be expecting us to read lots of old papers?' asked Rory. 'Because I'm not sure I'm going to be very good at that.'

'Oh, we'll be fine,' the Doctor told him. 'You read that bit of Menander, didn't you? It's a Time Lord gift, you can read anything, any language, as long as you're with me.'

'Wish I'd had that during my GCSEs,' muttered Amy.

'Anyway, it'll be fun,' continued the Doctor. 'You get to have your seaside holiday after all – all right, so without the sea, but with added archaeology!'

Amy started yawning. 'I'm sure I'll feel much more keen on reading ancient papers after a good night's sleep. That was a hint, Doctor,' she pointed out as he failed to move.

'Oh, right.' The Doctor shuffled backwards out of the tent. 'Night night, sleep tight. Don't let the bed-scorpions and snakes bite. See you in the morning!' The tent flaps closed on him.

None of them would have slept peacefully that night if they'd had any idea what the morning was going to bring...

CHAPTER 3

IT'S A JUNGLE OUT THERE

'Wakey wakey, rise and shine!' Amy sang out.

Rory yawned and pushed himself up on his elbows. 'What's the weather like?' he asked. 'I'm guessing sunny.'

'Well, let's go and see,' Amy replied.

She pushed open the tent door and looked outside for a few moments. Then she let the tent flaps fall and shuffled back inside. 'Tell me, did I just imagine that there was a desert outside when we went to sleep last night?'

'Er, no,' said Rory. 'You could tell it was a desert by all the sand.'

'Well, unless this tent turned into a TARDIS

during the night and flew off, something pretty weird's been going on out there.'

The two of them left the tent. 'Oh,' said Rory. 'Yes. That's a bit different, isn't it?'

'Doctor!' Amy yelled.

There was a rustling from the next tent, and the Doctor's tousled head appeared. His eyebrows rose in surprise. 'Amy, did you do this?' he asked.

'Of course I didn't,' she said.

The Doctor stood up, and the three friends looked around. They were surrounded by plants, thick-stemmed reeds with fronds fountaining out from their tops. The stems nearly reached up to Amy's waist.

'They look like papyrus plants,' said Rory. 'Except...'

'Except they're purple,' completed Amy.

'Doctor!' The two British archaeologists were coming towards them, pushing their way through the reeds. They looked very surprised.

The Doctor waved. 'Hello! Nice garden you've got here.'

'This is astounding!' cried Hunt. 'How could it have happened?'

'It's impossible!' said Grenfell. 'A plant that can grow in the desert – without water – and at such speeds – if I wasn't seeing this with my own eyes I wouldn't believe it!'

'I wonder...' murmured Hunt thoughtfully. 'Papyrus has so many uses. It can be turned into paper, rope, mats, shoes – even used as food. Surely this discovery will be of great benefit to the British Empire!'

'Well, that'd be nice,' said the Doctor. 'But don't count your chickens yet. I suspect there's rather more to this plant than meets the eye.'

Rory had been thinking. 'Doctor,' he said, 'you know that papyrus we saw last night? Well, that was a bit purple, maybe it was made from plants like this.'

'You mean the papyrus you spilled tea on?' Amy asked.

'Yes, I know, I'm a klutz, thanks for reminding me –'

'Shut up, Rory,' the Doctor said, interrupting. 'You might just be a genius.'

'I might?'

The Doctor was already striding away through the reeds. 'Come along, Ponds! And archaeologists, too. We're off to find Rory's purple papyrus.'

They pushed their way through the vegetation, heading for the cook tent where the papyrus had been taken. Several bewildered Egyptian servants joined them as they went.

A plant frond tickled Amy's chin and she brushed it aside. 'These are definitely getting taller,' she said. 'They must still be growing!'

'They probably are,' said the Doctor, 'but that's not the reason they're taller here. They're spreading out from a central source. These plants are older than the ones by our tents. And the ones right there,' – he pointed towards the cookhouse marquee – 'are even taller. Which means we're getting nearer to the place where it all started.'

Grenfell looked puzzled. 'But Gahiji has been in the cookhouse all night – why didn't he alert us to this?'

The Doctor stopped suddenly, flinging his arms wide to prevent anyone else walking past him. 'I think I have an idea why not. Go back, everyone. Amy, don't look.'

Amy ignored him, leaning over the Doctor's outstretched arm to look ahead. She could see a pair of sandals, with what looked like sticks lying on top of them. 'What is it?' she asked quietly.

'It looks...' said Hunt in astonishment as he circled round the Doctor, 'It looks like a mummy. A mummified body, I should say. But we've come across no tombs in our excavations, only documents.'

'And Ancient Egyptian mummies don't usually keep their clothes on,' the Doctor pointed out. 'I'm afraid we've found your suspiciously quiet servant.'

Amy drew in her breath in horror.

One of the Egyptians pushed past the Doctor. 'It is Gahiji!' he cried. 'My friend Gahiji, what has happened to you?' He knelt down beside his friend's body, pushing aside the clustered reeds with his hands. Amy could see Gahiji now. His face looked just like a mummy's. The yellowed skin clung tight to the bones of the skull, the nose resembling a mere fold of dry paper. It was a horrible sight.

'I would say,' began the Doctor, 'that every drop of moisture has been drained from that body.'

The Egyptian kneeling on the ground started to cry. 'What evil spirits have taken my friend from me?' he said – and then he yelled. The surrounding reeds had bent their leafy heads towards him; a swift, jerking movement like a cat that has suddenly sensed a mouse. He reached out to push them away, and the yell turned into a scream. 'It burns!'

The Doctor was there in an instant, grabbing him and dragging him away. 'Everyone – back NOW! RUN!' he shouted, and this time even Amy didn't dare to disobey him. The Doctor, the Ponds, the archaeologists and the few Egyptians who'd been with them all ran as fast as they could until they were back by Rory and Amy's tent, where the purple papyri were still only knee-high.

'Everyone inside!' called the Doctor.

It was a squeeze, but they all got in, the Doctor half supporting, half carrying the crying Egyptian.

'What happened back there, Nassor?' asked Hunt. 'Are you all right?'

In answer, the man held up his left hand. It was shrunken and withered, brittle skin clinging tightly to the fingerbones.

Rory, his years of nursing experience coming to the fore, sat down beside Nassor and tried to calm him. He gently examined the bony hand. 'I'm sorry,' he said at last. 'I don't think there's anything I can do. It's just... dry. Completely dry.'

'Like every drop of moisture has been drained from it...' whispered Amy, echoing the Doctor's words from earlier.

'Yes,' said the Doctor. 'I think we've found our water vampire. It's the plants.' He leant over and ripped two strip of cloth from the bottom of his robe, then wrapped one round each hand. 'I'll have a closer look. Everyone stay here.'

Of course Amy followed him anyway, so did Rory. They crept out of the tent, being extremely careful not to allow any flesh to come into contact with the reeds. The Doctor grasped a papyrus stem in his bandaged hand and tugged. Nothing happened. He got hold of several handfuls and pulled again. Still nothing.

Amy took hold of his waist and helped him pull. The plants stayed firmly rooted.

Rory took hold of Amy's waist and pulled too. Still no good.

'Anyone remember the story The Enormous Turnip?' said Amy. 'We need a little old man and a little old lady and a dog and a cat and a mouse before we're getting this baby out of the ground.'

The Doctor stopped pulling and stood up straight. 'No good,' he said. 'Rory, pop your head into the tent and see if anyone's got a pocket knife, will you?'

A few seconds later Rory handed a small silver penknife to the Doctor, who unfolded the blade – with some difficulty as his hands were still wrapped in cloth – and tried to saw through a reed.

To Amy's surprise, the knife cut straight through the plant's stem. 'Oh!' she said in astonishment. 'Oh, well that's all right then, isn't it? I mean, they probably don't have lawn mowers around here, but we could get a few scythes or something.'

But the Doctor shook his head. 'Look,' he said.

Amy looked. The Doctor had cut the plant close to the ground, but a shoot was already weaving its way out of the hacked-off stump. 'Cutting them down won't stop them. It won't help at all.'

Everyone was silent for a moment, then Rory said, 'I'm guessing the plants are alien, right?'

'I'm guessing that too,' the Doctor confirmed.

'And you think they have something to do with that papyrus document I spilled tea on?'

The Doctor nodded. 'The way I see it – and yes, I am guessing a lot of it but what you need to remember is that my guesses are always right –'

'Nine times out of ten,' put in Amy.

'Nine hundred and ninety-nine times out of a thousand,' corrected the Doctor, kneeling down to crawl back into the tent. 'As I was saying,' he continued once they were all inside, 'the way I see it is this. These purple plants somehow got seeded along the Nile river a few dozen centuries ago, where they grew alongside the papyrus plants. And because they were very similar to the papyrus plants, they got cut down and used in the same way.'

'But people in Ancient Egypt didn't get sucked dry like that poor man, did they?' said Amy.

'Maybe they did, maybe they didn't,' the Doctor said. 'If the plants were growing in the Nile, they were probably getting all the moisture they needed from that. Anyway, they were made into paper, and one of those documents ended up here. What you have to remember is that the whole point of the Oxyrhynchus excavation, the reason it's such an incredible find, is that the papers have been kept utterly dry for millennia. That's why they've survived. The purple papyrus was just lying dormant –'

'– and I woke it up by spilling tea on it,' completed Rory. 'Sorry about that.'

'Oh, don't be so hard on yourself,' the Doctor told him. 'On the one hand, you're a clumsy idiot, yes. But on the other hand, you might have helped to save the world. If it had happened some other time, when I wasn't around to sort things out, it could have been disastrous. OK, it looks like new plants are benign until they're fully grown – then they start reacting to water, and will take it from anywhere. Anywhere at all. And the human body is about sixty per cent water...'

'Shouldn't we be thinking about getting out of here?' said Amy.

The Doctor nodded.

'The other servants and helpers,' said Hunt. 'They must be warned!'

Rory was closest to the tent's entrance, and he was starting to move out when he stumbled and fell.

'You all right?' Amy began, then yelled as she fell backwards. The groundsheet beneath their feet was shaking.

A purple shoot burst through the floor of the

tent, then another, then another.

'Everyone out!' cried the Doctor as he hurried to Amy's aid. Rory, the two archaeologists and the Egyptians scrambled out of the doorway, but the papyrus stems were growing fast now and Amy and the Doctor couldn't get past.

'We're trapped!' said Amy. 'There's no way out!' Then she thought for a second and said, 'Oh right. We're in a tent.'

The two of them scrambled to the back of the tent and their fingers tore at the seams. The fabric ripped and they climbed through the hole.

'Amy? Amy?' Rory was calling but she couldn't see him. There was a wall of papyrus stems between them now.

'Rory?' Amy began to run along the outskirts of the camp, searching for a way through. The Doctor ran in the opposite direction.

They met on the other side of the circuit. 'I can't find a gap!' cried Amy. 'We need an axe – a machete – something to chop our way in! Ooh! Can't you sonic them?'

'That would be with the sonic screwdriver in my jacket pocket, would it?' said the Doctor.

'Yes!'

'The jacket pocket that's still attached to the jacket that's back in the TARDIS?'

'Oooooh!' Amy growled at him. 'So what are we going to do, then?' She jumped backwards as another reed pushed out of the sandy ground by her feet. 'The planet'll be overrun in a few hours!'

'Don't exaggerate,' the Doctor told her. 'It'll take at least a week. By which time we'll have thought of a solution.'

'By which time Rory'll be thin and crispy!'

'Hello?' Rory's voice came to them faintly across the sea of purple. 'Amy, Doctor, can you hear me? We're at the hut and it seems safe for now. The plants aren't coming inside. Yet. Er – any idea what we should do next?'

'Just stay safe,' the Doctor called back. 'Sit tight, and Amy and I'll be back later.'

Amy looked at him in surprise. 'Later? How much later?'

'Oh,' said the Doctor, 'about 2000 years later.'

CHAPTER 4

IN DE-NILE

'We're not just leaving them!' said Amy in amazement as she followed the Doctor out into the desert. 'I mean, that's not what we do, is it?'

'Of course not.' The Doctor waved away her concerns with a careless hand. 'But no point faffing about where no obvious solution presents itself, let's head for the source of the problem. We need to find out how they dealt with those reeds the first time round.'

'They probably wrote it down on papyrus,' said Amy. 'All we've gotta do is search through the millions of documents back there. Won't take us long!'

'Silly Pond,' the Doctor knew she was joking. 'We're taking a little trip in a time machine instead.'

Amy's face lit up. 'We're going back to ancient Egypt! Oh, that is so cool. Obviously, bad naughty reeds, big danger, all that stuff, but – ancient Egypt! That's more like it. Less rubbish and more pharaohs. Oooh, ooh, can we visit Cleopatra? The real one, I mean, not River Song.'

'Yes, that would probably be about the right time – and she might not recognise me – but to be on the safe side I'll aim for just a little bit earlier,' said the Doctor, looking concerned.

'Oh, you!' said Amy, punching his arm playfully. Then a few moments later: 'What, not really?'

The Doctor didn't answer.

Amy was really hot and thirsty by the time they reached the TARDIS. 'OK, ice-cold drink first,' she said as they entered the control room, 'then you do the coordinates and I'll do the clothes.'

'No, thank you, perfectly fine in my own clothes,' the Doctor told her, unwrapping himself from the white robes and putting his jacket back on.

Amy shook her head. 'Sorry, we did Ancient Egypt in Key Stage Two. I know all about it. One, I want the wig and the lots and lots of jewellery thing, and two, I want to see you in make-up.'

'I don't think –' began the Doctor.

'Lots and lots of make-up,' said Amy, deliberately ignoring him. 'I'm off to get the eyeshadow now.'

And with that she vanished further into the TARDIS.

A short time later, a rather grumpy looking Doctor operated the controls to open the TARDIS's main doors. He was dressed in a knee-length white tunic – sonic screwdriver tucked into the scarf tied round his waist – and his eyes were heavily outlined in black, with green powder on his eyelids ('To match your lovely green eyes,' Amy had said as she applied it. 'You wear eyeshadow now. Eyeshadow is cool.')

Amy herself, whose tunic reached to her ankles and who had definitely gone for the 'lots and lots of jewellery thing', looked altogether happier as they went out on to the sand. 'This is the same sand,' she said. 'Well, I know it isn't, but it looks like it. How about that? Back in time a few thousand years and the sand looks exactly the same.'

But one thing that very definitely didn't look the same was the river. As they approached it, it became very clear that this was no dried-out riverbed. 'Wow!' said Amy. 'That's what I call a pond and a half.'

'I think,' said the Doctor, shading his eyes and peering towards the high water, 'that we must have arrived near the beginning of Inundation.'

'Inun– what now?'

'"Key Stage Two", you said. "I know all about it", you said,' the Doctor remarked casually.

'Oh, Inundation, the Ancient Egyptian season where the Nile floods, that Inundation.'

'Yes, that Inundation. Which of course raises the issue of how we're going to get to the other side of this quite deep and rapidly getting deeper river.'

Amy looked along the river bank. 'We could

always borrow that boat,' she said. She looked up at the sky, which was pink with the dawn. 'Let's hope no one wants to go fishing before the sun's properly up.'

They walked along the bank till they came to the small fishing boat. Amy sat in it as the Doctor pushed it into the water, then the Doctor jumped in. 'Hey, is this boat made from papyrus?' Amy asked as the Doctor began to row. 'It looks all sort of reedy.'

The Doctor nodded. 'Not purple papyrus though. Which is lucky for us. And for the fisherman. Although...' He peered into the distance. 'Is it me, which it probably isn't as my eyesight is superb, or is that a purplish patch in the distance over there?'

Amy looked along the far side of the bank. 'Yup, I'd say that was a purplish patch. And I also can't help noticing that we're now heading towards it.'

It was true that the Doctor was paddling rapidly to change their course. 'Well, can't examine something without getting close, can we?' he said reasonably.

'As long as we don't get too cl– aaaargh!' There was a tremendous splash as Amy landed in the water. She was taken completely by surprise and for a few moments the impact and the cold knocked all other thoughts from her mind. Everything was suddenly cold and wet and she couldn't breathe.

As the shock faded, it became clear that air was needed in the very near future. Amy whirled her arms round, trying to propel her head upwards. She broke the surface with a gasp, and began dragging in huge lungfuls of air as she trod water. The Doctor was floating next to her, looking very surprised. The papyrus boat was upside down.

'What happened?' Amy spluttered.

The answer was a grunting roar. A huge, blunt-toothed mouth chomped down on the boat.

'Aaargh!' she yelled. 'A hungry hungry hippo!'

'Swim!' yelled the Doctor, as the hippopotamus chewed on.

Amy struck out towards the shore. Her long, powerful strokes were carrying her away from the hippo – but closer to the patch of purple reeds. She barely noticed it, all her energy was concentrated on the beast behind them.

She'd thought of hippos as dull, plodding, rather comic creatures that basked in the mud all day. There was nothing comic about this ferocious creature. 'What did we do to upset it?' she spluttered.

'Nothing! Just keep swimming! Nearly at the shore!' the Doctor called in reply.

But the hippo had left the wrecked fishing boat and was swimming after them. It was fast, and it was angry.

'Keep going!' the Doctor yelled.

Then, just as Amy thought those terrible teeth were about to sink into her wildly kicking legs, the hippo veered away from her. It ignored the Doctor too, and began swimming off in the opposite direction.

'What on earth –' Amy began and then realised where she was. The purple reeds were only centimetres away. She swam to one side, avoiding them.

The Doctor made it to the edge and scrambled on to the bank. Amy hastily swam across to him and allowed him to help her out of the water too. 'You OK?' he asked her. She nodded, still getting her breath back.

'What was that all about?' she said at last. 'Why did that hippo attack us, and why did that hippo stop attacking us?'

'It's an interesting thing. If you ask people what's the most deadly animal in Africa, possibly in the world, they'll say lions or maybe crocodiles. It's actually the hippo. Really very grumpy, hippos. Attack you for no reason, and don't give up easily. Which is the second interesting thing. It was almost as though it was afraid – of this.' The Doctor walked over to the patch of purple reeds, and bent over to look more closely at it.

'Not too close,' Amy said nervously. 'D'you reckon the hippo knew this plant is dangerous, then? By the way, your eyeliner's running.'

The sun was higher in the sky now, and they were beginning to feel the heat of an Egyptian day.

After the cold of the river, it felt glorious. 'At least we'll dry out quickly,' the Doctor said. He took the sonic screwdriver from his belt and shook it. Water dripped out. 'Won't be using that for a while.' He tucked it back in the scarf and pulled out a small black rectangle. 'Lucky the psychic paper's in a waterproof wallet.'

'Stop! Stop!' Angry voices came to them from the direction of the town. They looked up to see several men running towards them. The Doctor gave a friendly wave.

'They look crosser than the hippo,' Amy muttered out of the corner of her mouth. 'Do you think we ought to start running?'

'No, that would look suspicious, especially as they're yelling at us to stop,' the Doctor whispered back. 'Not that they've specified what they want us to stop, but I'm sure we'll find out very soon.'

They found out sooner than Amy would have liked. In a few seconds the men were on them. They grabbed the Doctor and Amy by the arms and began to drag them away. 'Thieves!' one spat at them. 'Low-lives! You take advantage of the death of the Nomarch to rob us of our sacred treasures!'

'I think there's been a slight misunderstanding,' the Doctor said. 'We weren't actually stealing anything.'

'What other reason could there be for your presence at the sacred spot?' said another of the men.

'Well,' the Doctor said, 'I can think of thirty-four reasons off the top of my head, not including the truth, which is that we didn't know it was a sacred spot, we just happened upon it, and anyway we were only looking.'

The man laughed. 'Well, you will not have to worry about "only looking" when your head has been cut off.'

Amy's eyes opened wide. 'When the what now? Cutting off your head for looking at a few purple plants? That's barmy.'

'You may be lucky. Perhaps they will only take your hands. Or whip you,' the same man said with a shrug.

'Yeah, that would be lucky,' said Amy. 'Look, we're friends of Cleopatra, you know! The Doctor's actually a really, really good friend of hers.'

'Quiet!' the Doctor hissed. 'Anyway, we're a bit earlier than that. But my friend's right,' he added loudly. 'We come from the pharaoh to pay his respects to your departed Nomarch. I, er, actually have a note from him here.' He waved the psychic paper that he was still clutching tightly in one hand.

The men stopped for a second and one took it from him. Amy got a brief glimpse of the paper: it was full of wavy lines and little drawings of eagles and lions and feathers and things. The man stared at it and shook his head. 'These symbols mean nothing to me. I will consult a learned man while you are prepared for judgement.'

'Is the psychic paper playing up?' Amy asked in a whisper. 'Did it get water in its works after all?'

The Doctor shook his head. 'No. He just can't read. Tricky script, Egyptian, there're more than 500 hieroglyphs.'

'Wow. Arm, owl, two reeds spells AMY. That's

all I remember from school,' Amy said. 'Don't remember learning about Nomarchs, though, what are they when they're at home?'

'Oh, governor, mayor, chief – that sort of thing. Bloke who rules the district. Egyptian big cheese. In this case, recently deceased Egyptian big cheese,' said the Doctor. 'That's probably made things a bit chaotic round here, which is going to make things either easier or harder for us.'

'I'm guessing, harder,' said Amy. 'Us and the easy option, they never go together.'

They were in the town now. If Amy hadn't known it was the same place she'd been in thousands of years in the future, she would never have guessed. There were mud huts painted white and there were tents, but there were also magnificent buildings and stone pillars. Above all, there were people. This was a bustling place, full of life, and she remembered the Doctor saying it had once been the third most important city in Egypt.

'This was the provincial capital,' the Doctor said, as if reading her thoughts. 'Sort of a New

York of the ancient world.'

They were shoved inside a mud hut. One man went off, taking the psychic paper away with him, while the others stood guard.

'So, the purple papyrus is sacred here, huh?' said Amy to make conversation.

'It would seem so. Not really a surprise. Gods everywhere you look in Egypt. Hundreds of 'em.'

'Yeah, yeah, I know,' said Amy. 'All creepy looking men with animal heads, birds and dogs and things. Because a man with the head of a dog is just the sort of being that everyone would look up to. D'you reckon he sniffs other gods' bums and pees up against sacred lamp-posts?'

'I think what you're doing there,' said the Doctor, 'is confusing the jackal-headed god Anubis with a Jack Russell. Easy mistake to make, of course, but you wouldn't want a terrier judging your worthiness to enter the afterlife.'

'All that stuff where they weigh your heart to see if it's too heavy to enter heaven sort of thing? I remember doing about that at school too,' Amy said. 'Basically, the Egyptian thing is, be nice or when you die a crocodile-lion-hippo thing will eat you up. Don't know about you, but I'd probably spend my life being nice if that was on offer.'

'Aren't you nice now?' asked the Doctor innocently.

She punched him lightly on the shoulder. 'What d'you think?'

Footsteps were approaching from outside. 'I think that if we're lucky we're going to get released now,' the Doctor said.

'We're usually lucky,' said Amy, but she didn't feel anywhere near as confident as she sounded.

She was right to feel worried. It looked like their luck had run out. The men who entered the hut were wielding swords. They looked pretty fierce.

'Nice to see you, I assume you've come to let us go,' the Doctor said, trying to get past them to the door.

He was pushed back roughly, and fell on to the floor with an 'oof'.

'Oi!' yelled Amy, but one of the men grabbed

her arm and pushed her down on to her knees. 'The traitors' death has been ordered,' he said, and raised his sword above her neck.

CHAPTER 5

DON'T WATER THE PLANTS

'Stop!' screamed Amy, as the man raised his sword. 'We're not traitors! Believe me, you're doing a really bad thing, the crocodile god'll eat your heart up if you hurt us, I am serious!'

Beside her, the Doctor was also struggling. 'You're making a big mistake!'

'Stop! Stop! Stop!'

'Stop!' Amy only just realised that someone else was shouting too. A male voice had joined in with her cries. She stopped shrieking and decided that it was safe to look up without risking bumping her neck on a sword blade.

A man in his mid-twenties had entered the

house. He had bronzed skin and a shaved head and he was holding the Doctor's psychic paper in his hand.

'These are honoured visitors who come from the pharaoh himself! Leave, now!'

The men slunk out of the hut without looking back. The young man held out a hand to help Amy get up. 'Please accept my heartfelt apologies at the way you have been treated,' he said. 'I am Khenti, scribe to the Nomarch.'

'The late Nomarch, would that be?' asked the Doctor, climbing to his feet.

Khenti nodded. 'As yet we have no new Nomarch. I continue to act as our Nomarch would have wished. And he would not, of course, have wished harm to come to representatives of the pharaoh,' – he glanced down at the psychic paper – 'the noble Doctor and Lady Amy.' He smiled then, and Amy felt a wave of liking for him. She would, she thought, have liked him even if he hadn't stopped her from being executed.

'Well, no harm done,' said the Doctor, taking

hold of his own ears and shaking his head from side to side. 'Yup, head still attached to neck. Do you regularly execute people within minutes of their arrival on no evidence without allowing them to defend themselves, though?'

Khenti lost his smile. 'We do not, noble Doctor. I am ashamed this has happened. The loss of Senbeb, our Nomarch, has upset the way of things. I have no doubt that a message got garbled in the telling and I can only apologise again.'

'Apology accepted,' said the Doctor.

Amy shrugged. 'I guess I've had near-death experiences that were closer to death than that. I'll let you off this once. As long as it doesn't happen again.'

Khenti seemed to understand the sentiment behind her words and his smile returned. 'I am glad. And I can assure you it will not happen again.'

'Well, let's keep our fingers crossed,' the Doctor said. He narrowed his eyes and stared at the young man. 'You know, you might be the very person to help us. How would you feel about a small chat?'

'I would be honoured,' said Khenti. 'Would you care to accompany me, noble Doctor – and of course, you too, Lady Amy, most favoured of Sutekh.'

The Doctor suddenly had a choking fit. Amy gave him a slap on the back. 'Hey, you OK?' she said.

'Just... er, what was that you said again, Khenti?'

'I remarked that Lady Amy, with her fair skin and hair of a sunset hue, must be greatly favoured by the god Sutekh who prized such things so highly.' Khenti looked worried. 'I trust I have not offended you.'

Amy glared at the Doctor. 'Nope, not offended at all. Don't know what's up with "the noble Doctor".'

'Oh, just someone walking over my grave,' said the Doctor. 'Let's go for that chat now.'

Khenti led them through the bustling streets. 'I have rooms in the Nomarch's house,' he said, as they turned a corner.

'Oh wow.' The house ahead was not at all what Amy had expected. More like a palace than a hut, it appeared to be made out of stone rather than the white-painted mud bricks found everywhere else. It had three storeys and what looked like a garden on top of its flat roof, sheltered with canopies.

Khenti led them round the side to a walled courtyard at the back of the house. 'Oh wow,' Amy said again. 'This is gorgeous.' Brightly covered tiles covered the ground. There were palm trees, and shrubs covered with heavily scented flowers. Geese ran across the yard, hissing and honking. What she thought at first was a swimming pool turned out to be a pond full of dashing, silvery fish.

'Gorgeous,' the Doctor echoed, flatly. Amy was surprised at his tone and turned to him with a frown. He pointed towards the pond. 'I especially like the little clump of sacred papyrus.'

Oh no. Amy looked over at the far side of the water. The Doctor was right, of course. While she'd been exclaiming at the beauty, he'd zeroed in on the alien threat. The cluster of reeds was very definitely purple. 'Great,' she said with a sigh. 'Get a lot of that round here, do you?' she asked Khenti.

He shook his head. 'The sacred reeds are very rare. And also very special.'

'Why?'

For answer, Khenti pointed over to the two boys who had just run out of the house. 'Nebi and Nubi, sons of the Nomarch. The gods sent the sacred reeds to save their lives.' He told the story.

'The boys had found a strange seed pod in the desert and had been playing "catch" with it. When it was accidentally thrown into the water they had jumped in to look for it. They didn't notice a crocodile swimming towards them...

'Living near the river, the boys had been able to swim almost since they could walk, and they swiftly swam for their lives, crocodile in pursuit. Escape seemed hopeless as the creature sped towards them in the water...

'Then out of nowhere the strange purple reeds had appeared, pushing their way through the surface of the river behind the boys. The crocodile had taken no notice, swimming on regardless. It swam into the patch of reeds...

'It made a hissing sound – angry, even scared – and then it just... stopped.' Khenti was silent for a few moments, remembering. Then he stood up and led the Doctor and Amy into the house. 'There,' he said.

Amy screwed up her nose in disgust as she looked at the thing. It had been a crocodile once. Now it was a desiccated thing of black and orange, its teeth still white and sharp but looking huge against its flattened head. If it was stood upright, nose to tail, it would be much taller than she was and the idea of meeting it in the water was terrifying.

'I guess we know why that hippo was scared of the reeds,' she said. 'Bad news like this would travel.'

'You were unlucky to meet an animal at all,' said Khenti. 'Most have avoided the river in the days since the happening. The sound of this crocodile's death lingers long in the mind. But not so long as the screams of the men who followed it...'

The Doctor looked up sharply. 'People have

died here?'

'Three men,' Khenti said. 'That very night. You would like to see them?'

'You've kept their bodies too?' Amy nearly screeched. 'What kind of sick joke is that?'

'I do not joke,' said Khenti seriously. 'They act as a warning to others. To touch the Water Thief is death. Even the Nomarch himself was not immune.'

'That's what you call it, the Water Thief?' said the Doctor. 'Interesting. Because thief implies it's taking something that doesn't rightfully belong to it, but if it's sacred it's doing the gods' will.'

'I think,' said Amy, 'that you've homed in on the wrong bit of what Khenti said just then. Even their big boss guy, the Nomarch, has been sucked to death by those purple papyrus things!'

But Khenti shook his head. 'No. That was not the manner of his death. The Nomarch had welcomed the sacred reeds, the saviours of his sons. But after the deaths of the men, his mind was changed. He declared them evil, and said they must be destroyed. That very day, the gods struck him down. On his wife's orders, I had some of the sacred reeds brought here to the palace, to be put in a place of honour so the gods would know we appreciated their gift and take no further revenge. The priest Hetshepsu has made it very clear that if harm comes to the Water Thief, harm will come to our city.'

The Doctor had screwed up his face while Khenti was talking, and Amy knew he was making an effort not to say something rude. 'I'll say one thing for the Egyptian gods, logical behaviour was never their strong point,' he commented at last.

'What about the people who brought the reeds here to the palace?' Amy asked hurriedly, before the Doctor could say anything that Khenti might find too offensive. 'How did they manage that without getting crisped?'

'The men prayed to the gods for their blessing and Hetshepsu, the priest, sacrificed a bull to the gods to win their favour. It was the gods' will that the men were dressed in garments of cow skin for protection until the Water Thief was safely in its sacred spot.'

'Leather gloves so their skin didn't touch the actual reeds. Very sensible,' said the Doctor. 'You know, getting everyone to dress head to foot in leather while those reeds are around wouldn't be a bad idea.'

Amy raised an eyebrow. 'Like an Ancient Egyptian biker gang? That'd give the archaeologists something to talk about back home.' She saw Khenti looking at her curiously and knew that to him she must sound like she was talking nonsense. Always a problem with time travel. She cast around for something else to say. 'Hang on a minute,' she said, 'your Nomarch – if he did something that the gods didn't like and they struck him down for it, what's that going to mean when he gets to the day of judgement? Will the crocodile-lion-hippo thing eat him? Er, sorry, that's probably a bit of an insensitive question, isn't it?'

She added the last bit because Khenti was looking extremely embarrassed by the question.

His coffee-coloured skin was turning redder than she'd have thought possible. 'We, his loyal subjects and friends, must hope that the many good deeds of Senbeb the Nomarch will lighten his heart enough to escape the hunger of Ammit and let him be conducted safely to the glories of the afterlife,' he said.

The Doctor was looking at the scribe through narrowed eyes. 'A very worthy thought.' He leaned forward. 'But I think there might be a little more to it than that. What don't you want to tell me, Khenti, hmm?'

Khenti gasped. 'I do not know what you mean.'

'Oh yes you do,' said the Doctor. 'You're scared to tell me something because you think I've – I mean, because I've come from the pharaoh and you're worried he wouldn't approve. You're worried you're going to get into trouble – and perhaps get other people into trouble too. You don't have to worry. I don't get people into trouble with the pharaoh unless I really, really have to. Your secret's safe with me.'

But Khenti shook his head, still bashful. 'Lord Doctor, I believe your words. But I must beg your pardon and your indulgence. It is not my secret to share.' There was a pause. Then he added, as though carelessly, 'Perhaps you would be interested in visiting Manu at the House of Beauty. It is a most fascinating place.'

'Fair enough,' said the Doctor. 'I might just do that, then.'

'Ooh,' said Amy. 'House of Beauty, can I come too? Cos being dunked in the Nile did not do good things for my make-up.'

Khenti's expression seemed to suggest he thought she had made a joke but wasn't quite sure what. Or why. The Doctor, on the other hand, was just smirking. 'Yes, they'd probably like having a living client to work on for a change.'

'Er, what?' said Amy. 'Oh great. You're going to tell me that the House of Beauty's where they pretty-up all the corpses, aren't you?'

The Doctor nodded cheerfully.

'Then I think I shall stay behind,' she said.

'It would be my pleasure,' Khenti told her with a bow.

'Don't water the plants,' the Doctor whispered in her ear as he passed her.

Yeah, right. Amy thought she was more likely to try hugging the hippo they'd met earlier than get close to those purple reeds. 'Good luck with your dead bodies,' she said.

The Doctor gave them a cheerful wave, and headed off in the direction Khenti had shown him. That left Amy and Khenti alone with only a mummified crocodile for company.

'Could we get out of here?' Amy said. 'That thing is really giving me the shivers.'

'Of course,' the Egyptian replied. 'In fact, I have been failing in my duty. As representatives of the Pharaoh, I should first of all have taken you to visit the Nomarch's family. Perhaps we should see them now – they are waiting for me to report on the plans for the party anyway.'

'Ooh, a party?' said Amy. 'Can I help? I love parties. Fancy dress is good, although I guess you can't go wrong as long as you have decent music and some nibbles. Got a theme planned?'

Khenti raised an eyebrow. 'Well, as it is a funeral party, the main theme will be the passage of the deceased into the afterlife.'

'D'oh!' Amy slapped her forehead. 'Right, OK, maybe not so much with the music and nibbles. Sorry.'

He laughed. 'But of course there will be music, the musicians are practising even now. There will be feasting also, and wine, and entertainments. Have you never been to a funeral before?'

'Er, yeah,' said Amy. 'Not quite so jolly as that, though. Has to be said, pretty miserable in fact.'

'I'm sorry,' said Khenti. 'Nevertheless, I would appreciate your help with the arrangements – if you are still happy to make the offer?'

'Yeah, go on then.' She linked her arm through his – a gesture he seemed surprised, but not unpleased, by – and led him towards the door. 'Let's go and say hi to the Nomarch's family. I'm guessing it's his funeral, right?'

'Indeed. I will introduce you to his wife. I mean widow. The Lady Emu.'

Amy tried very, very hard not to laugh. When Khenti asked her what the joke was, she realised she hadn't succeeded. 'I'm sorry,' she said. 'I don't mean to be rude, honest. But where I come from, being called Emu would be a bit like me being called "Duck Pond" or something.' She paused. 'Well, "Duck Williams", anyway. Don't want to upset Rory.'

'Rory?' asked Khenti.

'Oh. Yeah. My husband.' She felt a little twinge of pleasure that he looked disappointed at that.

'But your husband is not with you?'

'No.' She shook her head.

'He is busy elsewhere, then?'

Amy grimaced. She'd almost put it out of her mind – it was hard to remain connected to something that was so far in the future. But in a sense it was still happening right now too. Somewhere, somewhen, Rory was in terrible danger. And there was nothing she could do to help him.

CHAPTER 6
THE HOUSE OF BEAUTY

There was silence in the mud hut for a few moments after the Doctor's words died away. In was Hunt who spoke first. 'Your friends are abandoning us,' he said sadly. 'I cannot blame them. They must save themselves.'

'Oh no. No no no no,' Rory insisted. 'No, the Doctor and Amy wouldn't abandon us. I mean, Amy's my wife, and the Doctor is – the Doctor. Saving people is what he does. They'll be back.'

'Well, we mustn't rely on others for rescue,' said Grenfell. 'We are the leaders of this expedition, and we are responsible for those here. As well as for the knowledge that must be preserved for the world...'

His friend nodded. 'Absolutely. The first thing is that everyone must be warned not to touch the plants.'

A scream came from outside. Nassor the Egyptian jumped in terror. 'What is happening to my friends, my colleagues?' he cried.

'I think they've found out about the plants for themselves,' said Rory. He gasped and stumbled. 'What was that?'

'An earthquake!' cried Hunt. The tightly packed mud floor was cracking and heaving.

'The papyrus is trying to break through,' said Rory. 'We need to find somewhere safer. Any ideas?'

Grenfell nodded. 'Yes! I have it! Even these fearsome weeds would find it hard to get through stone. And there is –'

'– the ruined palace!' Hunt completed. 'Yes, of course. It's only really a floor with some fragments of wall still standing, but it's big enough to house everyone. But how to get there?'

Rory was about to take a swig from his water

bottle, but stopped with the bottle just touching his lips. 'We can use this,' he said. 'We can decoy them away from the path.'

He sprang into action. All of them had water bottles. There were a number of clay pots with stoppers, holding a variety of goods. Rory emptied them all out, not bothering what mixed with what on the floor, and put some water into each. The others, grasping what he was doing, started to help. Anything liquid that could be found was pressed into service and poured into a clay pot.

Rory had more preparations to make. He pulled off his white robes – the others stared in some surprise at the shorts and T-shirt he was wearing below them – and started to wrap the cloth around his hands. 'Everyone do this,' he said. 'Make sure there's no bare flesh for the plants to touch. That'll buy us time.' His last act was to fashion a megaphone out of a piece of stiff cardboard. 'Mr Hunt, you shout out and see if you can make some of your workers hear. Tell them what we're going to do, and get them to do the same, then pass on the message to others. If they haven't got water they need to try to join up with someone who has. We'll all meet at the palace.'

Hunt passed on the message. As he was yelling out of a window, the first purple shoot made it through the hut's floor.

'I think that's our cue to move,' said Rory. 'Everyone ready?'

The others nodded, determined looks upon their faces. The two archaeologists were wearing the kid leather gloves they used to handle documents, and trousers were tucked into socks to stop plant fronds tickling their ankles. The Egyptians had used torn strips of robes to protect themselves as Rory had.

'Right then – here goes!' At the door of the hut, he hefted a stoppered clay pot in his hand. 'OK, plants – fetch!' He flung the pot into the sea of purple on his left and listened for the crash. Like a cornfield blowing in the wind, the reeds swayed towards the source of the sound. Rory heaved another pot to the right, and was relieved to see a number of reeds sway back in that direction. Between the two sets of reeds, something resembling a path began to take shape. Rory took a deep breath, and dived for the gap. The others followed, throwing pots to either side. Each time a pot crashed open, the plants bent towards the moisture.

At last the ruined palace came into view. It was really little more than a few stone blocks piled here and there on a stone base, but their hearts lifted at the sight of their sanctuary. More workers from the dig were heading in from other directions. They all collapsed, panting, on a flight of stone stairs that led nowhere.

'I feel like I've run a marathon!' Rory said between gasps. 'What I'd really like now is a nice drink of water. Pity about that.'

'Your idea has saved us all for now,' said Grenfell, 'and I'm very grateful. But you make a good point. Without water, we may not last here for very long.'

Rory nodded. 'I know. Let's just cross our fingers that the Doctor gets back soon.'

Thousands of years earlier, the Doctor was paying a visit to the House of Beauty. Despite its grand name it was actually a fairly plain looking tent. Would he find answers there? He hoped so.

The first thing he found in there, however, was a body. He'd been expecting that, as he knew this was where the dead were prepared for what was to come. What did give him a slight shock, though, was seeing a jackal-headed man brandishing a vicious-looking metal hook at him. He took a step back in surprise, but the creature began to speak. 'Hello!' it said in a rather muffled voice, and waved with the hand that wasn't holding a weapon.

'Hello,' said the Doctor. 'I'm the Doctor.' He held out the psychic paper. 'I've come from the pharaoh.'

'My name is Manu,' said the jackal without moving its mouth. 'I am the chief embalmer.' The human hands reached up and pulled off the jackal-head mask. 'Thank you for honouring me with a visit.'

'Oh, no problem, like to see everything that's

going on. I'm here to pay the pharaoh's respects to the late Nomarch and...' He looked at the body on the table, 'I'm guessing this is him right here.'

Manu nodded enthusiastically. 'I have washed the body,' he indicated a large tub of perfumed water, 'and now am about to begin the process.'

'Mind if I stay and watch?' the Doctor asked.

'It would be a honour, oh guest who comes from the pharaoh,' said Manu with a bow, narrowly avoiding sticking the hook up his nose. 'Whoops, not my nose it's meant for!' he said. He bowed again, putting his hands behind his back this time. 'Please, remain as long as you desire.'

Manu put the jackal mask back on and the Doctor watched with interest as the embalmer stuck the hook up the corpse's nose and wiggled it around. 'Just mushing up the brains a bit,' Manu said. 'Easier to get them out through the nose that way, it takes ages if you pull them out lump by lump.'

'I thought you preserved the person's organs,' said the Doctor. 'So they could use them in the afterlife.'

'Only the useful ones,' Manu said with a laugh. 'No point keeping hold of something as pointless as the brain. What good's a brain ever done anyone?'

'Right. No. Good point,' said the Doctor. He helped Manu turn the body over so the liquid brain drained out of the corpse's nose. 'Look at all that useless grey matter. Why would anyone even bother having it?'

'Indeed,' said Manu, as he wiped up the brains. He rolled the body back over, then picked up a black stone knife and made a slit in the belly. 'Now, let's get those insides outside!'

The Doctor sniffed. An odour had wafted up from the knife-cut, and not one that was usually associated with dead bodies. The scent of bitter almonds. 'Now that's interesting,' he said. He was even more interested to see that the corpse's internal organs were a distinctive shade of pink.

'Oh, I have seen the insides come in all shapes and sizes and colours too!' Manu said as the Doctor frowned over the body. 'You soon learn, in my job, that no two people are alike.'

'But the pink colour – the smell – does that not mean anything particular to you, then?' asked the Doctor with a frown.

Manu looked puzzled. 'Smell?'

'Don't worry about it.' The Doctor moved away. 'I'm going to head off now. I'll pop back in and see how things are going later, if that's OK?' Khenti had obviously expected the Doctor to discover something by visiting the embalmer, and it looked like he'd discovered it pretty quickly.

Bright pink innards, a bitter almond smell – these were signs that death was due to cyanide poisoning. An accident perhaps, or even suicide? Possible, but unlikely. No, the Doctor would be willing to bet his remaining lives that the Nomarch had been murdered. Not struck down by the gods, but killed by some human agency.

The question was, though, how did Khenti know about it? Was he the murderer? No, surely not, confessing murder to a supposed representative of the pharaoh, however sympathetic, would be a rather foolish thing for a killer to do.

The Doctor also didn't want to believe he'd left Amy alone with a murderer.

And aside from all that, what did it have to do with the Nomarch being allowed into the afterlife? He'd already made his views on Egyptians and logic known, albeit mildly, but that one definitely didn't make much sense.

'Thank you for your visit,' Manu said as the Doctor turned away. 'I hope I will have the pleasure of meeting you again before you depart. I will have finished here in perhaps a few hours' time.'

The Doctor stopped still. 'Finished? You mean finished this first stage of the embalming?'

'No.' The Doctor swung back round to see the embalmer shaking his head – or rather, to see the jackal mask wagging from side to side. 'I will have completed the process.' He laughed to see the Doctor's expression.

'Not getting the joke, I'm afraid,' the Doctor said. 'It normally takes a month or two to dry out a body – ah.' He let out a sigh of understanding.

'That's what Khenti was hinting at. Not the mur– I mean, I get it now.' Best not to mention murder. It seemed suddenly probable that he was the only person who knew about it. Well, he – and the murderer. 'I wonder,' he continued to Manu, 'would purple reeds be part of the process here, by any chance?'

'Well...' The mask hid Manu's face, but the Doctor could imagine the expression and was sure he'd hit home.

'I think it might be worth my while to hang on here for a bit after all,' said the Doctor.

CHAPTER 7

ARM, OWL, TWO REEDS SPELLS AMY

Amy thought that if only she could get the idea of Rory and what might be happening to him out of her mind, she would be enjoying her trip to Egypt. She liked Khenti, and now she also liked Emu, the Nomarch's widow.

Emu was in her thirties, much darker skinned than Khenti, and her black hair was arranged in an elaborate style with gold chains and jewels woven into it. She wore a lot of jewellery and her eyes were heavy with make-up, but Amy didn't detect any vanity there – it was society that demanded the richness of the dress, not the woman herself. The fact that when they entered the room, Emu was sitting on the floor playing some sort of board game with the two boys, Nebi and Nubi, added to the impression that this was someone who wouldn't stand on ceremony.

The widow had jumped to her feet as Khenti and Amy approached, and seemed pleased to meet the visitor. Her sons were sent off with their nurse, a jolly elderly woman called Banafrit, and Emu clapped her hands and asked a servant to bring refreshment for everyone. This turned out to be barley beer served in pots with straws – a bit bizarre to Amy's eyes, but it turned out the "straws" were strainers to sieve out the lumps. She was glad of the drink, though, as she wasn't sure what to say to the newly widowed woman. After their cups were empty, Khenti asked Amy to excuse him while he filled in Emu on the funeral arrangements to date. Amy turned to leave, but Emu motioned for her to stay. 'These matters are not secret,' she said. Amy noticed a tear running down the lady's cheek, which was quickly brushed away.

Amy suddenly felt hopeless. What was she

doing here? Intruding on people's grief, for what purpose? They were no nearer any answers. OK, the TARDIS in her usual clever way had taken them back to the right time – the time when the purple papyrus appeared. They'd discovered that it sucked the water out of living things. Well, they had a pretty good idea of that already.

What they hadn't found out was any way of dealing with the reeds. In fact, the one man who'd tried to get rid of them had been struck down dead, which wasn't particularly encouraging.

Rory could be facing death now, and here she was, sitting in a lovely palace with nice people drinking lumpy beer.

'Aren't you scared?' she said suddenly, interrupting Emu and Khenti's discussion. 'Aren't you scared that there's a deadly plant here and you've brought it into your home?!'

Emu smiled a little. 'It is safer for us to show it honour than not to do so. And we give offerings to the sacred Water Thief, we have done so every day since my husband left us.'

That sounded ominous. 'You don't throw young maidens to the plants, do you?' Amy asked in horror.

'Merely cattle.' Emu laughed at Amy's face. 'Don't worry, Khenti hasn't lured you here to be a human sacrifice.'

'Well, I'm grateful for that,' said Amy. 'I'm trying to keep my brushes with death to under two a day. It's tricky, but I'll get there in the end. After being nearly beheaded this morning I'd rather not have to deal with being sacrificed this afternoon.'

'I don't understand,' said Emu. 'Nearly beheaded? Did you meet with bandits on your journey here?'

Amy explained and Emu was horrified. 'It is true that the sacred reeds are not to be approached, and that the penalty is death. But it is not for peasants to decide upon or administer that penalty.'

'Well, they didn't,' said Amy. 'They ran off to ask someone, and then came back ready to go for the chop.'

Khenti was frowning too. 'I didn't realise that,'

he said. 'I thought the men were acting rashly, I had no idea that someone had sanctioned their act. The peasant who brought your documentation to me made no mention of anyone else being consulted.'

'Oh great, now we've got a mysterious enemy.' Amy groaned, then a thought struck her. 'You don't think the Doctor could be in any danger, do you?'

'Where is your friend?' asked Emu.

'He's at the House of Beauty,' said Khenti. 'No harm should come to him there.'

Amy sighed. 'This is the Doctor we're talking about. Harm could come to him anywhere. And in a spooky place full of corpses...' She trailed off, realising that she was probably talking about Emu's husband. 'Look, I'd feel happier if I could go and find him, would that be OK?'

'Of course. I will show you the way.' They said goodbye to Emu, and Khenti led Amy out of the palace, back through the gardens – complete with sinister purple reeds that made her shudder – and back into the town. 'We will take a short cut through the marketplace,' Khenti said. 'I did not tell your friend this way because it is harder to describe, but it will get us there quicker.'

They turned a corner into the marketplace.

Amy screamed.

Things were getting interesting. The Doctor was trying to remember if he'd ever been present during an embalming before. He didn't think he had. Any chance to pick up new knowledge was always welcome.

After removing the lungs, liver, stomach and intestines – but not the heart, because, as Manu told the Doctor, it contained a person's self and would be needed for judgement in the afterlife – the embalmer had placed the organs in canopic jars. Then, with leather gauntlets protecting his hands and arms, Manu carefully picked up an armful of purple reed stems and placed them over the Nomarch's body.

The Doctor watched with interest. 'You've not done this before?' he asked Manu.

The embalmer shook his head, making the

jackal mask wobble comically once more. 'Not on a man, no. I tried it out on a monkey that was found dead in the fields, and it seemed to me that nothing could be simpler.'

'You could be right,' said the Doctor. 'I think it's starting...'

The process had begun. The reeds lying on the stomach moved, falling inwards as though the corpse had taken a particularly deep breath in. The skin of the chest sunk, clinging now to the ribs. Reeds rolled off the table as the arms shrank into sticks, and the Doctor jumped back so he wouldn't come into contact with them. The face was the last part of the body to be affected. Although the skull held the shape of the head, the features collapsed like a popped balloon.

In very little time, the man was completely mummified.

'What now?' asked the Doctor.

'I will pack the body and oil it, then wrap it in strips of linen,' said Manu. He was beaming. 'This is going to revolutionise the embalming process!

What took days can now be done in minutes!'

'The fast-track to the grave,' said the Doctor. 'You'll have so much time off you won't know what to do with yourself. So, tell me – was this your idea, then?'

Manu looked just as sheepish as Khenti had done when the subject had been brought up earlier.

'It's a good idea,' said the Doctor encouragingly. 'Saves everyone a bit of time. Don't have to wait months for the funeral. People can get on with their lives...'

'That's not why she's done it!' Manu burst out, then quickly shut his mouth.

The Doctor rolled his eyes. 'I'm not here to make trouble for anyone!' he said. 'You can trust me. Honestly, you can. I'm here to find something out, that's true. But not this. I just want to know everything in case it may be relevant – or to make sure it isn't. Well, that and because I'm nosey. Can't help that, sorry. Although it must be said my nose now isn't a patch on what it used to be. I'm guessing that "she" is the Nomarch's widow, am I right?'

The embalmer nodded reluctantly.

'And from what Khenti said, this idea of using the reeds might have something to do with the judgement in the afterlife, am I getting warm now?'

Manu nodded again.

'So assuming she's acting in the best interests of her husband, which I have no reason to doubt, could we skip the twenty questions and have you just tell me what's going on?' said the Doctor.

Manu sat down, nearly knocking over a jar full of intestines as he did so. He righted the jar and took off his Anubis mask, putting it on the floor by his feet and sighing. 'Oh, very well. The Lady Emu's plan was this. It is usually more than a month – perhaps more than two – before the departed has to face Anubis and be judged for the deeds of his life. By that time every deed has been recorded within his heart. The lady knew that our Nomarch was a good man, and his heart should weigh light on the scales against the feather of Ma'at. The gods had chosen to punish him for his act of defiance with death. But if he could go immediately to judgement –'

The Doctor almost laughed. 'He could be judged before that final deed weighed down his heart. That's brilliant! Mad, but brilliant. She's using the powers of this papyrus to try to trick the gods!'

'Indeed.'

'You're not worried that doing this might weigh down your own heart? That the gods might not look kindly on someone trying to trick them?'

Manu said with simple dignity, 'I trust the gods would know that I act out of respect and love for the Nomarch's widow.'

'Well, let's hope so,' said the Doctor. 'I –'

And then he heard Amy scream.

The Doctor instantly dived for the door – but his foot caught on Manu's discarded jackal mask and he went flying. He put out his hands to save himself...

...and landed on the reeds that had spilled off the table.

CHAPTER 8

THE PENALTY OF THE PEACH

The Oxyrhynchus workers had arrived at the ruin with disturbing tales. Although many of them had reached safety through Rory's water-bomb idea, they had all seen people lost to the deadly reeds. The two archaeologists spoke and understood the native languages well, but Rory suspected they didn't pick up on the tiny nuances, the little expressions of fear or grief that were tearing at his heart. Sometimes the gift of translation turned out to be a curse.

But Rory was a nurse, and he'd been used to coping with other people's fear and grief even before he'd met the Doctor. He began to check over the milling men; some had cuts and bruises and sprains and he dealt with those as best he could.

The trouble was – and he felt very selfish for thinking it – there weren't nearly enough injuries to keep him busy. Soon he would be forced just to sit, and wait. And also to have to try to avoid as much conversation as possible that could lead to him saying, 'Yes, actually I'm a nurse from the future'.

He knew the Doctor would act differently. The Doctor wouldn't just sit on the stone floor of a ruined building, trapped by purple reeds. He'd find a way out.

But Rory wasn't the Doctor. He was just going to have to be patient.

It wasn't going to be a lot of fun.

Things happened very quickly. The Doctor was falling – he fell – he landed – he felt a tug on his hands, a vacuum-cleaner-on-the-skin type of sensation – and then he suddenly felt very, very wet. Again.

He scrambled to his feet, noted Manu standing over him with an empty tub that he vaguely remembered had once held perfumed water, and ran to the door. 'Thank you!' he called over his shoulder. 'Very grateful to you for probably saving my life but Amy's in trouble!'

Outside the House of Beauty he looked around anxiously. He saw a flash of red hair in the distance and he ran towards it. There was Amy, the scribe Khenti beside her, and in front of them...

Raised on a stone plinth were three figures. Once, probably, they had been human. Now they were little more than skeletons covered with skin. One was kneeling down, the others were bent forward, twig-like arms outstretched, reaching for something that was no longer there.

'I thought they were coming for me,' Amy said as he reached her. 'I know, stupid. Laugh at me, why don't you?'

'Not today,' said the Doctor. 'Mummified bodies in the middle of the street, anyone could be forgiven for a bit of screaming.' He turned to Khenti. 'These would be the gentlemen who tried to steal or otherwise appropriate the sacred papyrus, I take it? And here they are in all their glory to scare people into leaving the plant alone.'

Amy put up her hand. 'Yup, you got me, I'm scared. Believe me, I will not be touching that plant. But there again, I wasn't planning to anyway. And by the way, you smell nice.'

The Doctor frowned at her. 'I don't think my odour is the thing at issue here.'

'Yeah, but it's nice.' Amy leant over and sniffed his hair. 'You could market that. Eau de Doctor. And talking of water, have you been for another swim in the river?'

'No. But I have been finding out some interesting things. For example –' he turned to Khenti – 'did you know that the Nomarch had been murdered?'

The scribe's mouth fell open. 'What? Surely that cannot be true.'

'Not only can it, but it is. The Penalty of the Peach, I believe it's called here.'

'The what now?' Amy wrinkled her nose. 'That doesn't sound so bad. In fact it sounds quite nice. Peaches, soft, juicy, peach-coloured, that sort of thing.'

'And with stones full of cyanide,' the Doctor told her. 'Interesting thing, cyanide. Kills you quickly. Has a very distinctive scent of bitter almonds although funnily enough, most humans can't smell it at all.'

'Very interesting,' a new voice said.

They span round. Amy gave a gasp. A very tall, shaven-headed Egyptian was standing behind them. He was almost skinny enough to be mistaken for one of the mummified bodies on the plinth and his eyes were as black as skull sockets.

The Doctor, of course, didn't jump to conclusions about people, but it wasn't the man's creepy smile or the way his bare feet had crept up on them so quietly that made him certain this was an unpleasant person. He just knew, the way he knew that it wasn't a good idea to trust a Dalek or take tea with a Krillitane.

The skinny man bowed. 'Honoured visitors. I am Hetshepsu.'

'The priest. Right,' said the Doctor. 'I'm sure we're honoured to meet you too. Aren't we, Amy?'

'Er, yes. Of course. Very honoured,' said Amy, who was still staring at the newcomer with a wary expression on her face.

'But it's probably time we were getting on with something,' the Doctor continued. 'Do excuse us.'

Hetshepsu nodded, but Khenti looked concerned. 'Doctor, we surely must discuss –'

The Doctor cut him off. 'Later, Khenti. Later.'

'Very well.' Khenti gave them a short bow. 'I am sure the Lady Emu would wish me to offer you the hospitality of the Nomarch's palace. Would you do us the honour of dining with us this evening?'

'Love to,' said the Doctor. 'Now come on, Amy.' He took hold of her shoulders and steered her towards the House of Beauty.

She pulled back as they got nearer. 'Is that the dead-people tent? Not sure I fancy that just at the moment, thank you very much.'

'OK. We'll go and look at something else,' said the Doctor. 'Let's go and see some traditional old Egyptian crafts.'

Amy frowned at him. 'Hang on, are we on a school trip or are we investigating alien reeds so we can save Rory in the future? Just wondering.'

'We're supposed to be visitors from the pharaoh. We've also just discovered that murder's been committed here and we don't know who we can trust,' he said. 'So let's behave as unsuspiciously as possible for now.'

'I know who the murderer is,' said Amy. 'Definitely that Hetshepsu guy. Creepy or what?'

'Don't judge by appearances,' the Doctor told her sternly. 'Ah, here we are!'

'"Traditional old Egyptian crafts"?' said Amy. 'They're making a coffin! Is everything here about death?'

'Pretty much, yeah,' said the Doctor. 'Well, that's not quite fair. They put in a lot of effort to ensure a nice afterlife, though. Think of it as taking out a kind of post-mortem pension plan. They make the coffins human-shaped so they can act as a body in the afterlife if they're needed. They'll also make sure it's placed in the tomb with those eyes painted on it facing east, so it can see the sunrise.'

One worker was painting a face on a wooden mask. 'I guess that's supposed to be the Nomarch,' said Amy. 'He looks younger than I'd expected.'

The Doctor smiled sadly. 'Here, you'd be considered middle-aged. Someone twice your age would be elderly. The ancient world wasn't the safest or healthiest of places. Mind you, doesn't matter how old or ill you get, if they make you look young and healthy on the mask, you'll be young and healthy for all eternity.'

'Wow,' said Amy. 'Take that, plastic surgery. But can we talk about the you-know-what now?'

They moved away from the craftsmen who were carving, painting and sticking things together.

'What are we supposed to do?' Amy began when they were at a reasonable distance. 'Do we have time to do the whole Sherlock Holmes thing?'

'We have to,' said the Doctor. 'I'm going to go back to the House of Beauty first. Check I've not missed anything. You don't have to come, though.'

She shook her head. 'You'll laugh at me,' she said. 'I don't want to. I'm not squeamish, but – well, I just don't want to watch. You go do your CSI bit, though. I'll be fine.'

'You're missing out on a bit of living history,' said the Doctor enticingly. 'Well, OK, dying history, but it amounts to the same thing.'

'You sell it so well,' said Amy. 'I suppose it's different if you're a thousand years old. All these tiny human lives must seem like mayflies to you.'

For a moment the Doctor didn't answer. He was staring into the distance. Without looking at her he said 'Is that how you see me? Is that how I appear to you?'

Startled by his serious tone, she reached out and took his hand. 'I didn't mean it like that. I didn't mean that you don't care. I know you care – more than anyone else I've ever met. I'm sorry.'

'"Any man's death diminishes me, because I

am involved in Mankind",' the Doctor quoted the words of John Donne. 'But you were right. Sometimes I can't let myself care. The times when I've felt it, really felt it – they're the times when I've wondered about going on. Or, sometimes, they're the times when I've tried to change things, and that can be really bad news for the universe. Don't forget that when you travel in time, it gets very complicated.'

Amy walked over to the wooden coffin, reached out a hand and touched the painted wooden face. 'You mean... today I don't want to see this man dead, because I've talked to his wife and I know someone killed him and it's all raw and sad. But if we'd landed a century ago I'd never have heard of him. If we'd landed last week, I might have shaken his hand. And back where Rory is, in the future...'

'You'd visit the Nomarch in a museum without a second thought.'

'Mm.' She smiled. 'I'd've still found it a bit creepy, though.'

To her relief the Doctor finally met her gaze

and smiled back. 'Fair enough. But you see why we have to investigate this murder. Can't leave a murderer running loose. Whether someone lives for fifteen or fifty years might not make much difference in a few centuries' time, but today – today it means a lot. It means grieving relatives and a life cut short and I'm not going to let that happen if I can stop it. OK?'

'OK. I'll go back to the palace,' Amy said. 'See if I can pick up any info there – we might get a clue from what the Nomarch had to eat and drink.'

Drink! It was all Rory could think about.

They'd had no food or drink since the previous evening. There was very little roof left of the palace and Rory had stayed huddled in one corner when possible, trying to keep out of the fierce sun. Being medically trained, he could recognise the signs of dehydration. His head hurt and his mouth was dry. Everyone was getting irritable and snappy, which was also a symptom of dehydration, but could also be because they had been trapped together for the whole day.

At least the terrible heat should be fading soon, taking with it the fear of heat stroke. But if the Doctor wasn't back soon...

Rory wasn't sure they'd last another day – and he felt that it was his fault. He was cursing himself for bad judgement. The palace had seemed like a sanctuary when Grenfell and Hunt suggested it – but Rory should have thought quicker, suggested they head for the town boundaries instead. OK, so they'd have had to keep moving to outrun the reeds, and they would be in the desert which was not known for its water or food, but at least they wouldn't have been trapped. There might have been a chance for them out there somewhere, whereas here – well, he couldn't see that they had a chance at all.

It wasn't that Rory doubted for a moment that the Doctor and Amy would succeed in their mission and come back for him. He just thought it likely they might not come back in time.

Rory buried his head in his hands. Hunt moved

over to him and spoke in a low voice. 'Courage, my friend,' he said.

Rory looked up and shrugged. 'I'm not scared,' he said. 'Just not sure we've done the right thing.' He explained.

Hunt shook his head. 'Of course my first thought was to leave. But more would have lost their lives trying to get outside the town, thc distance was too great. And you saw how quickly those reeds spread. Even those who made it in the first dash would have been overcome by now. No, this was the best course of action for us all. We have at least survived thus far, which means there is still hope.'

But how much hope was there really?

A shout came from somewhere among the massed workers. A man jumped to his feet and arms reached up, trying to pull him down again. 'Yafeu, no!' men were crying.

'Yes!' shouted the man called Yafeu. 'I will not remain here to die! I am going to find water!' He pushed his way through his fellows, shaking off clinging hands.

'No, come back!' yelled Rory. 'You'll die out there!'

'I'll die in here!' Yafeu shouted back. 'I will not sit here waiting patiently for the end, like a sheep waiting for slaughter!'

Rory, Hunt and Grenfell all got to their feet but they weren't able to get close to the fleeing man. They had barely pushed a metre or two through the crowded ruin by the time Yafeu had vanished into the twilight. They were only about another metre further on when they heard him die.

'Sleep,' said Grenfell, turning back with a shudder. 'The sun is setting and we should sleep now. We must be ready to face the challenges tomorrow will assuredly bring.'

Rory sighed and agreed. He glanced around at the stone walls, trying to imagine the place as the palace it had once been. His thoughts drifted to the banquets that would have been held there, the wine, water and beer that would have been consumed...

No. He shut his eyes and tried to shut off his thoughts too. That way madness lay.

CHAPTER 9

CSI: EGYPT

Amy headed back to the Nomarch's palace. She deliberately took the short cut through the market, so she could pass the three mummified thieves on their plinth and prove to herself that she wasn't squeamish.

The market was almost completely deserted, and she realised it must be nearly evening by now. The day had passed in a blur, and she was feeling pretty hungry. Then she looked at the plinth with its horrific death sculpture, and suddenly stopped feeling hungry after all.

She made herself stand close to it and study it in detail. The man who had been kneeling had black hair that hung in straggly strands around the grotesque skin-covered skull. He was wearing only a linen loincloth, now flapping loosely around his waist, and every single rib could be seen in his bare chest. The two standing men she thought must have had shaven heads, like the majority of the Egyptians she'd met. Now, however, with the skin shrunk tight to the skull, a tiny amount of hair had pushed its way through. One man's head showed a gingery fuzz nearly as red as her own hair, the other's skull was peppered with black stubble.

What had sent these men to the purple reeds? What had made them grasp such an ugly death? Had they been acting for good or for ill? Were they taking orders or had they decided to do it for themselves?

The answers would probably never be known, and she wouldn't discover any more by staring at the corpses. Amy considered that she'd now conclusively proved her lack of squeamishness, so she could go on to the palace with a clear conscience. And maybe a little shudder. And maybe walking really quite fast.

She was concentrating so hard on not being bothered by the bodies that when she arrived at the palace she headed for Khenti's office and walked straight in.

Khenti and Emu jumped apart quickly.

It took a second for Amy to grasp that they'd been kissing. When she did, she turned round and hurried out, calling 'Sorry,' over her shoulder.

Khenti caught her up as she reached the pond. 'Amy! Wait! Please!'

She put up her hands. 'Hey, I'm not judging. I snogged someone the night before my wedding, what a woman does before her husband's funeral is up to her.'

'I'm not ashamed,' he said, looking her in the eye. 'I have always admired the Lady Emu, as the wife of my employer. And it seemed that she occasionally smiled upon me. She has been wonderful, this last week, hiding her heartbreak as best she can for the good of the city. But tomorrow, she must say her final farewells...'

'And she got all upset and you were just comforting her and before you knew it you were kissing,' Amy completed. 'I said, I'm not judging! It's OK!'

But it wasn't OK. Because what Amy had suddenly realised was that here were two people who had a motive for murdering the Nomarch. Hey, they could have been responsible for her and the Doctor nearly being beheaded when they first arrived...

No. She shook her head at that unspoken thought. Khenti or Emu, they were two of the people that the blood-thirsty men might have consulted and who might have issued the orders to behead them, that was true – but it was Khenti who stopped the blows falling, it was Khenti who'd saved their lives.

So, not responsible for that little bit of fun. But the death of the Nomarch – well, she couldn't be sure about that. She'd have to tell the Doctor.

Khenti had been watching her face anxiously, trying to trace her thoughts through her rapidly changing expressions. Now she laughed to see him. She linked her arm through his and drew him to the edge of the fish pond. They sat down, Amy letting her feet dangle in the cool water. Khenti had been carrying a carved wooden box under his arm, and he put it down by his side, resting a hand on it.

'Honestly. It's OK,' she said, as he still looked worried. 'Come on, you'll make some girl a lovely husband one day. And if it turns out to be Emu, then she's the lucky one.'

Khenti dropped his eyes in mock-sheepishness. 'Lady Amy, you flatter me,' he said.

She'd never liked him more than at that moment. No, she wouldn't mention it to the Doctor after all. So Khenti might have a motive for killing the Nomarch, but she was certain he would never have done it; certainly not in such a sneaky, underhand way as using poison. Khenti could never be a murderer. He –

There was a cracking sound. She felt a hard thump on her back and suddenly she was underwater.

Splashing her arms around, she tried to propel herself back to the surface, but strong arms were holding her down. She tried to shout, but water just flooded into her mouth.

She couldn't get free, she couldn't breath...

Amy realised with horror that she was about to drown. Khenti was trying to kill her – and he was going to succeed. She would never escape from the water.

'Water!' Rory woke up and realised he'd shouted out loud. He'd dreamed of water, of the palace banquets with their overflowing jugs and goblets. But that wasn't all he'd dreamed of...

Hunt had stirred when Rory cried out, and now Rory put a hand on his shoulder. 'Wake up!' he hissed.

'What is it?' asked the other blearily. Then, waking fully, he sat up with a start. 'What's happening? What's wrong?'

'Nothing,' said Rory under his breath. 'Don't wake up everyone! Listen, I've had an idea. This was a palace. It had to get its water from somewhere. Did they have wells in Ancient Egypt?'

Hunt nodded. 'Yes! Yes, they did!' His face fell. 'But where one might be I have no idea.' He turned to where his colleague still lay asleep and put out a hand to wake him. 'Grenfell may know.'

In whispers, they explained Rory's idea to Grenfell. To Rory's immense disappointment, the other archaeologist also knew of no clue to where a well could be found. 'And if it had been fed from the river it might be dry now anyway,' he said.

Rory screwed up his face. For a few brilliant moments he had thought he'd found a solution. Now it looked like the Doctor was their only hope after all.

But Grenfell was looking thoughtful. 'I don't know of a palace well,' he said. 'But I do recall mention of a fishpond in the palace courtyard. I saw a bill for marble for the floor and sides.'

'Yes!' Hunt agreed. 'You're right! I know the document in question.'

'A fish pond would have dried up long ago,

though,' said Rory.

'Perhaps – but perhaps not. If it was fed by an underground stream, one that was not connected to the river – it is possible the source is still there.'

'Well, what are we waiting for, then?!'

The sun had not yet fully set, and there was enough light for them to work by. The small courtyard was stone, just like the palace floor, and although reeds had crept up through some cracks it was still a reasonably safe place to be. The three Englishmen began trying to prise up the stones, but only succeeded in making their fingers bleed.

'We need to get the men,' Grenfell said.

Hunt wasn't so sure. 'It may give them false hope. We have no idea if there really is water down there.'

'No, Grenfell's right,' said Rory. 'We need their help. And the hope may not be false. Just giving them any hope at all might be enough for now.'

I'd rather die doing something, he thought, than die sitting around waiting.

But, he added to himself, I'd rather not die at all...

'I thought the wrapping of a mummy took weeks,' said the Doctor, watching as Manu shovelled sawdust into the slit he'd previously made in the Nomarch's abdomen. 'Is this another one of your "Get Judged Quick" schemes?'

Manu chuckled. 'I am acting on the instructions of the Lady Emu, yes. Once I have reshaped the body with this stuffing,' – he waved around his wooden scoop, sending a cloud of sawdust over the Doctor and making the Time Lord sneeze violently – 'I will wrap it swiftly in linen. While I will observe the necessary rituals, of course, any delay could prevent the Nomarch from entering the afterlife. Hetshepsu is not in favour of this, I must tell you. But the Lady Emu has insisted.'

'Hmmm.' The Doctor tried to frame his next question in an "I'm just interested, nothing sinister going on here" way. 'Must be interesting, all the things you found out. For example, you could probably even tell me what the Nomarch had to eat last, having removed his stomach and... and everything,' he finished, with a casual wave of his hand towards the canopic jars that held the Nomarch's insides.

Manu laughed. 'Yes indeed. Although I could probably have told you anyway. Pomegranates! The Nomarch's favourite fruit.'

'Nothing else?' asked the Doctor.

'Nothing that was... obvious,' said Manu, which the Doctor took to mean nothing undigested. So the only thing the Nomarch had eaten shortly before his death was pomegranate.

Having discovered what he wanted to know, he could have left. But Manu's job was fascinating, and the Doctor found it hard to drag his eyes away. Manu worked swiftly and skilfully; he was clearly a master craftsman. The Doctor sank into a chair and gave himself up to watching the process.

Having shaped the body to his satisfaction, Manu wrapped it in a simple cloth shroud, then turned to what looked like several hundred bedsheets-worth of white linen. He recited incantations as he began to bandage the shrouded form.

'I never thanked you properly for your quick

thinking earlier,' the Doctor said after a while.

'Oh, it was nothing,' said Manu, not looking up from his work. 'Indeed, you cannot really call it quick thinking, as I barely did any thinking at all! My hope was that the Water Thief would steal its water from an easy source before turning to a living being.'

'Well, it worked. And I'm extremely grateful.' The Doctor sat there for a few moments, frowning. 'I'm wondering if you might have found something that's going to save a lot more people...' he muttered under his breath. 'That would be nice.'

Would it work – on a larger scale? Possibly. He wasn't sure the Water Thief's behaviour had been entirely consistent – but then again, he had seen it at so many different stages that it was hardly surprising there wasn't much of a pattern.

When the Nomarch's sons, Nebi and Nubi, had thrown the seedpod into the river, the reeds had shot up straight away. Despite having access to a whole river-full of water, the plant had still drained first a crocodile and then the men who had tried to steal it. It was newly grown, however, and as desperate for water as a newborn baby is for milk.

One thing these reeds didn't do was multiply everywhere, not like those on the future Oxyrhynchus site. But then those ones were relatively safe until they were fully grown. Perhaps having a river – or a pond – full of water meant there was no need for them to spread out.

So the ones in the future were spreading out, searching for water – but they were also much, much weaker without that water to sustain them. From memory, the future papyri were skinnier – ha, weedier! He laughed at his own pun – than those he'd seen here in Ancient Egypt.

What about the cut reeds, the ones Manu had used for the mummification process? Well, they had had their source of water cut off – but they'd been fairly sated already. He'd been safe for those few moments until Manu had doused them. Once they started to dry out, however...

'Where are the reeds?' he asked the embalmer.

'The ones you used earlier to dry out the body.'

Manu looked up, surprised. 'I placed them in a box and the scribe Khenti took them back to the palace,' he said. 'He said he might have need of them, but I am hoping that the Lady Emu will give me permission to use them again in future.'

'I wouldn't count on it,' said the Doctor, jumping to his feet. 'Sorry to keep rushing off, but I think I need to be somewhere else.'

He dashed out of the door. Those reeds would be drying out by now, and they'd want water again. They'd want to root again. Khenti might not realise just how dangerous a burden he was carrying – and by now, Amy would be with him.

CHAPTER 10

ARE YOU MY MUMMY?

Amy couldn't breathe. Her whole world was water. The pressure on her back was forcing her down, down...

And then it was gone. Strong hands were pulling her up. She broke the surface, coughing and spluttering. Her vision was blurred and wet, but all she could see was – purple.

'Amy!' That was the Doctor's voice, calling for her. She blinked rapidly, trying to clear her eyes, hoping that the coughing would stop so she could call back to him.

'Over here!' Another voice – Khenti's. It was very close, and she realised it was his arms that were holding her above the surface of the pond. She pulled herself out of his grip, and her vision and voice finally returned as she turned to face him.

'What d'you think you're doing?! Were you trying to kill me?'

He shook his head. 'Lady Amy, no! I was trying to save you – from the plants.'

She turned back to the side of the pond. Purple papyri were waving over the edge, dipping into the water.

The Doctor skidded to a halt at the far side of the pond. 'I think he's telling the truth. I had a bad feeling something like this was going to happen. Is that the box you were keeping them in?'

Amy followed his gaze. The carved wooden box that Khenti had put down beside them was split open and reeds were sprouting from it. 'I heard it,' she said. 'I heard it crack open. That was what made the noise just before you pushed me into the pond.'

'I didn't have time to warn you,' said Khenti. 'The Water Thief was shooting towards us, I had to get you out of its path. It was leaning into the water, I thought it was going to get you...'

'And so you were holding me under the water so it couldn't reach,' Amy realised.

'Only for a few moments,' said Khenti, 'until I was able to propel you further away from the edge.'

Only a few moments. It had felt like hours. It had felt like forever. It had felt like her entire life.

'Thank you,' she said.

The pond was shallow enough for her feet to reach the bottom, but she struck out and swam to the other side where the Doctor was waiting. He reached out his hands to pull her up. Khenti waded over and hefted himself out beside her.

'The reeds – it's like back at...' Amy trailed off, realising that there was no way of completing that sentence without Khenti thinking she were mad. But of course the Doctor knew what she meant without her having to put it into words.

'They want water,' he said. 'If they're thirsty, they spread out until they find it.'

'But these were cut stalks – dead things,' said Khenti.

'I don't know how it works!' said the Doctor in an exasperated tone. 'They're rooting themselves, they're sending out spores – I've no idea! In the absence of a fully equipped laboratory – or at least an electron microscope and a hazmat suit – we're going to have to go by guesswork. Just keep out of their way, and keep them in water.'

Amy looked over to the other side of the pond. The patch of purple seemed bigger now. 'Doctor,' she said. 'I think they're still spreading.'

He nodded. 'Right. No more risks. They'll stop spreading if they're in water. Probably can't uproot them, as we couldn't before, but let's give it a go. Khenti, I need those leather gauntlets that were used to bring the reeds here in the first place...' He stopped, frowning. 'They brought a whole clump of reeds, roots and all,' he said.

Khenti agreed.

'Then it's likely the plants only root themselves firmly on land. Sending their roots down as far as they can go, trying to get to any water that's below the ground. They don't need to do that if they've got an adequate water supply. Right, slightly amended plan. Khenti, leather gauntlets as before. Amy, get me a bucket and spade.'

She boggled at him. 'You're not going to try to make sandcastles again, are you?'

'That,' he said with a grin, 'is precisely what I am going to do.'

Amy ran to the market, this time hardly glancing at the three mummies on display. She'd seen some of the traders using wooden scoops to serve out grain into pots, and thought both scoop and pot would be ideal as the nearest Ancient Egyptian equivalent to a seaside bucket and spade.

Something was niggling at the back of her mind as she took what she wanted from an unattended stall, but she couldn't place what it was.

By the time Amy got back to the palace courtyard, the Doctor was dressed up in his plant-approaching armour. The reeds were still spreading. The Doctor had ripped up the tiles that surrounded the pond, revealing the bare earth beneath.

Now he took the "spade" from Amy, and began to dig a narrow trench from the very edge of the pond.

'What are you doing?' she asked.

'Rory wouldn't have needed to ask, he's a sandcastle expert,' the Doctor said. 'I'm digging a moat, of course. You dig a ditch round your sandcastle then extend the channel down to the sea and let the water fill it up. Only my castle is this clump of plants and my sea is that garden pond. Now go and help Khenti make sure everyone keeps out of the way.'

She didn't have to. The windows of the palace were full of people peering out to see what was going on, and it was clear that they weren't intending to get any closer than that. So Amy stood and watched the Doctor as he dug his way around the reeds. He was making it deep, and the pond water was flowing further along with every shovelful.

'Done,' he said at last, standing back.

The whole patch of plants was enclosed within

the "moat".

'I get it,' said Amy. 'The reeds'll end up in the water, whatever direction they're growing in. Then they'll stop spreading.'

'That's the plan,' the Doctor agreed. He leaned closer and whispered in her ear. 'Just keep your fingers crossed, will you?'

She crossed her middle and index fingers and waved them at him.

Khenti joined them and the Doctor explained what he'd done. 'Does everyone know not to come near?'

'Oh yes,' said Khenti. 'They have all seen what happened to the first thieves, they will not attempt to approach the plants.'

'That's it!' Amy shouted. 'I knew there was something wrong, something I'd seen out of the corner of my eye. Doctor – one of the mummies is missing!'

Amy, Khenti and the Doctor hurried back to the empty market square. Amy was half hoping she'd been mistaken, embarrassing as it might have been to admit it, but no. Only two figures were on the plinth now.

'No one would dare to touch them,' said Khenti.

'Well, he didn't just walk off on his own!' said Amy. 'At least, I hope not.'

The Doctor had been scanning the market place. Now he pointed to a tent to one side. 'Looks like something over there,' he said.

They hurried over. Amy had a sudden rush of déjà vu as she once again saw a twig-thin leg sticking out of a doorway. 'Yes. Here it is,' said Khenti, looking down sadly on the mummified figure.

Amy screwed up her face. 'What sort of mad idiot carries off a mummy? "Oooh, I know what my tent needs; a dried-out corpse would really improve the decor."' Having previously proved she wasn't squeamish, she didn't feel there was any need to look too closely at the body again. In fact she was determined not to. But it was like having an itch that mustn't be scratched – the urge became irresistible. She looked at the mummy. And then looked again, more closely.

'This isn't the same one,' she said.

'Don't be silly, Pond,' said the Doctor.

'Oi! I am not being silly. This is a different person – mummy – whatever.'

The Doctor and Khenti stared down at it.

'Are you sure?' the Doctor asked.

'It had red hair. Now it hasn't.'

Khenti was peering at the skull. 'Lady Amy, you can barely see the hair on this man's head, it is shaven. I think you must be mistaken. Perhaps it looked different in the light of the sun to in the gloom of this tent.'

Amy was beginning to doubt herself now. 'Yes,' she said reluctantly. 'I guess you're right.'

Khenti glanced up at the sky. 'Speaking of the sun, it is getting very low. We should return to the palace if we are to eat with the Lady Emu tonight.'

CHAPTER 11

THE BOOK OF THE DEAD

Back at the palace, a meal had been prepared and was waiting for them. 'We have been eating only simple food in this time of mourning,' Lady Emu said. 'All my servants are busy preparing for the great funeral feast tomorrow. I hope this does not displease you.'

'Oh no. No, that's fine,' said Amy, who was actually quite relieved. She'd been worried she might have to eat hippo or something, whereas the dishes of bread and fruit actually looked rather appetising.

She wasn't so pleased to see their fellow guest at the meal – the priest, Hetshepsu. A servant showed

Amy to a chair next to him, but the Doctor offered her his chair instead. Amy gratefully accepted, and it was the Doctor who sat down beside the priest, while Amy sat by Lady Emu. Khenti sat slightly apart on a cushion on the floor. 'What are you doing down there?' Amy asked. 'Come and sit with us!' She waved at an empty chair.

He gave her a puzzled smile. 'You are very gracious, Lady Amy, but you offer me an honour I do not deserve. I am only a scribe here, remember.'

Amy sighed. She'd put her foot in it again.

The servants were handing round food. Amy helped herself to a handful of dates and figs. The Doctor took a pomegranate and scored round the peel with a small knife, then twisted the fruit open to reveal the glistening red seeds inside. 'I love pomegranates,' said the Doctor. 'My very favourite fruit.'

Lady Emu smiled sadly. 'It was also the favourite of Senbeb, my husband.'

'Then I hope he had eaten many of them before he began his trip to the afterlife,' said the Doctor.

'It would be a comfort to you to know his belly was full and he was content.' Amy stared at him. There was making conversation, and there were creepy inquiries about what your dead husband had been eating.

Oh. Right. She got it, he was looking for clues to the murder. 'Yeah, it would be good to think that,' she joined in.

Luckily Lady Emu didn't seem to think the subject was weird. 'I am afraid not,' she replied. 'That thought would have given me comfort indeed. But Senbeb had eaten nothing since his morning meal of bread and honey.'

'Ah. Well. Never mind,' said the Doctor.

The rest of the evening was taken up with small talk and some discussion of the funeral arrangements. Hetshepsu would be conducting the ceremony.

'Did you receive delivery of the Book of the Dead my scribe has prepared for the Lord Senbeb?' Lady Emu asked the priest.

'Indeed,' he said, with a nod to Khenti.

'I'm sure you agree it is something very special,' she said.

'Oooh, really?' That was the Doctor. 'You know, I wouldn't mind a look at that. Would that be all right?'

'I would be honoured,' replied the priest. 'Perhaps you would accompany me back to the temple after the meal?'

'Oh yes,' said the Doctor looking him straight in the eye. 'I would be honoured.'

After everyone had finished eating, the Doctor reminded Hetshepsu of his promise. 'Let us go now,' the priest said. 'If that is acceptable to the Lady Emu.'

'Of course,' Lady Emu said. 'We have prepared rooms for both you and Lady Amy, Doctor. The servants will take you there when you return.'

'Thank you.' He turned to Amy. 'Don't wait up,' he said. 'But I will be back. Don't worry.'

He stood up before she could say anything and followed Hetshepsu out of the room.

At the temple, Hetshepsu offered the Doctor a seat, and then went to fetch the scroll.

'Here,' he said, handing it over. 'The Book of the Dead that will be used for the Nomarch's ceremony, then placed in his tomb.'

The Doctor took it. 'Lovely,' he said. 'And such a pretty colour. Unusual. Why would that be, I wonder.'

Hetshepsu spread his hands wide in a gesture of ignorance.

'Oh, I'm sure you know. It's written on papyrus made from the sacred reeds, which I think you're very interested in,' the Doctor explained.

'Of course,' said the priest. 'I am a servant of the gods, so the things they send to us are always interesting to me.'

The Doctor nodded. 'I'm just wondering how interesting. And how important. And how far you'd go to stop someone who wanted to get rid of those sacred reeds? And then, how far you'd go to stop someone you thought might have an even higher authority – or who might find out what you'd done?'

'I don't understand,' said Hetshepsu with a puzzled smile. 'But wait, I am forgetting my manners. I will fetch some refreshment.'

He went out of the room. Quickly, the Doctor grabbed a reed pen off a table and dipped it in a jar of ink. By the time Hetshepsu returned, he was sitting back on his chair as if he'd never moved.

'Let me offer you a drink,' said the priest.

The Doctor shook his head. 'No, thank you.'

'Really?' Hetshepsu looked surprised. He put down the jug and the bowl of fruit he was carrying, and picked out a large orange-red sphere from the bowl. 'Then may I tempt you with a pomegranate? You said they were your favourite.'

'No, thank you,' said the Doctor again. 'Definitely not a pomegranate.' He jumped to his feet. 'Well, I'd better be going. See you tomorrow at the funeral. Bye!'

Back at the palace, a servant showed him to a room on the first floor. A few minutes after he'd sat down on the carved wooden bed, Amy popped her head round the door. 'Knock knock, can I come in?' she said.

He patted the bed and she came and sat down beside him.

'I didn't get a chance to tell you earlier,' she began. 'Don't really want to tell you now, actually, feels like telling tales. But there's this thing between Khenti and Lady Emu...'

The Doctor tutted. 'Oh, you humans and your love affairs.'

'Oi, Mr Dismissive! I'm not gossiping, I'm telling you they could have had a motive to murder the Nomarch!'

He frowned. 'Oh, didn't I tell you? I know who the murderer is. Nothing to worry about.'

Amy opened her mouth several times, and finally said, 'You what? Were you planning to tell me at any point? Who is it?!'

'The priest. Hetshepsu. Obvious when you think about it. Someone who can read, someone with an interest in sacred stuff – and, biggest clue of all, he looks really creepy.'

Amy looked extremely put out and the Doctor laughed.

'Are you having a joke with me?' she said. 'Just because I said I thought he was the murderer?'

'You were right! You should be pleased.'

'So what are we going to do now?' Amy asked.

The Doctor shrugged. 'Well, if I were you I'd go and get some sleep. Hetshepsu's doing the funeral service tomorrow. We'll wait till that's out of the way then have words.'

'You're making it sound like he's the local vicar opening the village fete!' said Amy. She sighed and stood up. 'Oh well, if that's what you think's best...'

Amy went out of the room and the Doctor looked around. What to do now? No point wasting time with sleep; he still had to work out what do about the problem of the purple papyrus.

There was a bottle and a golden goblet on a small table by the bed. He picked up the bottle and sniffed it. 'Fruity,' he said aloud. 'Pomegranate wine. Don't mind if I do.'

He poured some of the pink liquid into the goblet and raised it to his lips.

The wine was already going down his throat when he detected the scent of bitter almonds.

CHAPTER 12

THE WEIGHING OF THE HEARTS

Grenfell and Hunt had woken the workers. Many were tired and sick and had not wanted to get up, but once the plan had been explained to them even the weakest of them began to dig. A few stones were prised up then used as levers to raise more.

Hours passed, the temperature dropped and the moon rose, and still they dug. There was earth underneath the stones, but under the earth they'd found tiles, and the archaeologists expressed an opinion that this could be the layer where the pond had once been. Of course, even if this were the case they would have to dig deeper still to reach the water source.

So they dug on. Men fell, sick from thirst, but others took over. Then they too would become too weak to work, but those who had rested would take up the challenge again. Even Nassor, who had only one working hand, took a turn to dig – and it was he who first gave the cry 'water!'

For a moment, Rory thought he'd imagined it. The word "water" was a constant refrain inside his head, it took a second for him to realise someone else had said it out loud. But others were taking up the shout. 'Water! Water! Water!'

It wasn't water, Rory discovered, it was only liquid mud. But that was something – more than something – it proved water was there to be found.

Everyone had a new lease of life suddenly. They dug and dug as fast as they could – and they had their reward. The water, when they reached it, was still closely related to mud, but it was drinkable – and there was enough for everyone. There were risks in drinking it, Rory knew – cholera, typhoid, other waterborne diseases – but if the alternative was dying of thirst or, now the sun was rising again, heatstroke...

He made his decision. He drank.

Even the iced ambrosia he'd drunk on Phintus Beta was as nothing compared to this cocktail of warm water and dirt. Rory gave a very contented sigh.

Of course, now his thirst was quenched, he was really beginning to feel hungry...

They dragged the Doctor into the room and held him there, his arms still in their grasp and his knees scraping along the floor. In front of him was a set of scales, two brass saucers suspended from a centre pillar taller than he was.

Crocodile-headed Ammit watched eagerly as Anubis approached the Doctor. She did not want the Doctor to pass the test. She wanted to feast.

Anubis had the head of a jackal but the hands of a man. Yet they felt like talons as they reached into the Doctor's chest and ripped out a heart.

'The heart contains all your deeds, good and bad,'

he boomed. 'Is your heart heavy with bad deeds or light with goodness? It shall be weighed against the feather of Ma'at so judgement can be made.'

The feather of Ma'at was on one side of the scales. The Doctor's heart was tossed on to the other side. The scales began to wobble up and down – heavier, lighter, heavier, lighter...

They were settling now. The Doctor stared hard, as though he could influence the scales with his gaze. He knew, none better, how many deeds weighed heavily on his heart. Yet he had always tried to do right – would that be enough to save him? 'The road to the underworld is paved with good intentions,' he murmured to himself.

A tiny bit lighter, a tiny bit heavier... the scales steadied. They stopped.

His heart was just lighter than a feather.

The Doctor went to breathe a sigh of relief, then remembered he had no breath. He was dead now. A passing thought wondered why he hadn't regenerated, but then he'd always suspected that wouldn't work forever. Sometimes things went wrong.

Ammit turned her crocodile head away in disgust. Beautiful Ma'at was smiling, however. She held out a hand to the Doctor to conduct him to the eternal pleasures of the afterlife – and Anubis roared 'STOP!'

He reached out towards the Doctor again. A moment's agony, and Anubis held the Doctor's second heart in his hand. He threw it on to the scales – and the scale pan sank. A metallic clank as it hit the floor, the heaviest heart ever seen.

'One heart records the good deeds, one records the bad,' growled Anubis. 'Ammit may devour both of them.'

The crocodile's jaws opened wide. Snap, snap, the hearts were gone. She turned to the Doctor, jaws wider than ever, and lunged at him –

The Doctor sat up. 'Wow,' he said. 'I thought I was dead.'

Amy glared at him. 'So did I,' she said, sounding furious, but the Doctor saw her brushing tears away.

Everyone at the palace had been up early, preparing for the day ahead. Amy had wandered sleepily downstairs and found herself getting in people's way. She was surprised not to find the Doctor there and wondered if he was out investigating something or other.

Lady Emu had already left, leaving a message with the servants that her guests would be welcome to join them at the funeral. Khenti had also gone. After helping herself to some bread and fruit, Amy had finally decided she'd better check the Doctor's room, just in case.

That was when she found him on the floor, not moving. She didn't want to think about the minutes that had followed.

'Clever,' said the Doctor, when he'd recovered a bit and was sitting on the bed. 'Poison in the goblet, not the wine. Must have done it even before we had dinner – he'd overheard me talking about murder so he already knew he was in danger. Wouldn't have been hard to find out what room they were giving me.'

'But how did you survive?' Amy asked. 'Cyanide – it's totally deadly!'

The Doctor grinned at her. 'Luckily enough, I've been poisoned before. Long story, country house, Agatha Christie was there, let's not go into it now.'

'And that's lucky?'

'Mm hmm. Because my body already knew it could deal with it. Just a matter of fighting, and it had had practice. Added to that I realised what it was extremely quickly and only swallowed the tiniest drop.'

'OK.' She sat down on the bed too. 'What are we going to do now? Your would-be murderer's off at the funeral parade, along with everyone else in the city.'

'Well, we'd better join them,' said the Doctor. 'Although...'

'What?'

He looked suddenly serious. 'Let's not let Hetshepsu know we're there, OK? Just in case. But I have an idea for that...'

Twenty minutes later, a brightly painted jackal head popped round the door of Amy's room. 'Woof, woof,' it said. 'Got it! Knew there'd be a few at the House of Beauty. How do I look?'

Amy narrowed her eyes and peered at the Doctor as he came through the doorway. 'Well, apart from your skinny white-boy body that has obviously not been living under the Egyptian sun for years and years, you look fine. How about me?'

She held up Lady Emu's bronze hand mirror. It was hard to see clearly in the shiny yellow metal, but her reflection looked reassuringly unfamiliar. The long black wig hid her own hair completely, and the heavy makeup disguised her features. She'd found a wrap of Lady Emu's that went round her shoulders, and with golden cuffs and bangles covering her arms and a jewelled collar around her throat, her tell-tale pale skin was barely noticeable at first glance.

'You'll do,' said the Doctor. 'Come on – better get running if we're gonna catch up with that coffin...'

Now Rory and his companions were no longer thirsty, other problems had raised their heads. Hunger of course, and heat, and impatience. Grenfell and Hunt, although chiefly concerned about the fate of their workers, could occasionally be found gazing wistfully into the middle distance as they wondered about the fate of their many manuscripts, somewhere out there in their biscuit tins.

The manuscripts! Didn't that mean things were going to be OK? The Doctor knew all about the archaeologists, knew too about all the manuscripts they'd found. Surely he could only have come across that information in the future if everything was all right now.

Rory sighed. It was a comforting thought, but somehow he was pretty sure things weren't that clear cut with time travel.

He wandered into the courtyard. After the first frenzy, where everyone had been so desperate to get at the water, things had calmed down. Now some people were sleeping while others worked to enlarge the hole to the underground stream; later they would swap roles.

All around the courtyard, the alien papyri could be seen, growing taller and taller. They hadn't yet penetrated the stone floor of the yard or the palace itself, but Rory wasn't convinced their haven would remain safe for much longer.

In fact, even as he was thinking that, it was getting more dangerous. 'The death plant! It is here!' The cry came from the bottom of the ditch. Men were scrambling to get out, pulling rocks and earth down on themselves in their haste.

Rory pushed through the fleeing workers and stared down the hole. At the bottom was a tiny shoot of purple. A spore from long ago that had suddenly found itself in the light? A reed that had found its way from outside the palace to this spot? He didn't know. How it had got there didn't really matter. But there it was, its roots greedily taking in the water that should belong to the men who had found it.

In their search for water, they had exposed themselves to their original foe – the bare earth was no barrier for the papyri, and the water would draw them there. Rory briefly considered trying to replace all the stones, but they didn't have the tools to do the job well enough to stop the reeds breaking through. Their best option was to retreat.

He followed the men back into the palace and once more settled down to wait for the Doctor. 'Please hurry up, Doctor,' he whispered.

CHAPTER 13

DEATH AT A FUNERAL

'Hurry up, Doctor!' Amy was worried they wouldn't reach the funeral in time. Luckily the desert procession was not fast-moving, and a bit of jogging brought them to the rear of it. They could see the brightly coloured coffin on its ox-pulled sled, small in the distance ahead, and began to make their way through the throngs of mourners to get closer. A line of servants walked behind the sled, carrying all sort of things – chairs, jars, baskets of fruit, pairs of sandals – that would be placed in the Nomarch's tomb for his use in the next world. 'I'll give you a hand,' said the Doctor, taking a bowl of pomegranates from a heavily laden servant. 'Yeah, me too,' said Amy, relieving another man of a bottle of date wine. They mingled with the members of the procession, gradually getting closer and closer to the front, and by the time they reached the tomb itself they were near to the coffin.

The coffin was taken off the sled and stood in the opening of the tomb. Two men in Anubis masks held it upright. Thin trails of sweet-smelling smoke spiralled down from bowls of burning incense and curled around Lady Emu and her sons as they came forward to drape garlands of flowers around the coffin's neck, large, brightly coloured blooms that Amy didn't recognise.

Two priests walked up to the coffin. One of them was easily recognisable as Hetshepsu, even though Amy couldn't see his face. He held a small metal instrument in his hand, a tool a bit like a flattened axe. The second priest unrolled a scroll of papyrus.

Amy reached out and grabbed the Doctor's arm, pulling him closer. 'Do you see that? It doesn't look papyrus-coloured to me,' she hissed into the jackal mask's ear.

The mask wobbled up and down as the Doctor nodded. 'Lilac,' he said. 'That scroll's been made out of the purple papyrus.'

'So why isn't that priest sucked dry? Why aren't there reeds popping up all over the place?'

The Doctor shrugged, making his mask almost fall off. He hurriedly pushed it back into place. 'If you'd been cut, woven and pounded flat, you'd probably not feel up to much either. In that state, I suspect it needs a taste of water to remind it of what it's missing, get it to pull itself together and start growing. And I have an idea it's not going to get that for a couple of thousand years.'

'Oh!' Amy stared at him. 'You mean, it's the papyrus from the future? The one that started this whole mess?'

He nodded. 'It was a Book of the Dead. I saw that before Rory christened it with tea. And the other thing I saw...'

'Yes?' said Amy.

The Doctor gave her a huge grin. 'The other

thing I saw was that at the bottom of the scroll someone had scrawled "Dear Doctor, here are the coordinates you need, love from the Doctor".'

Amy stared. 'You left yourself a note?'

'That's how we got here. To exactly the right time and place.'

'I thought it was just the TARDIS being clever,' said Amy.

'No,' replied the Doctor evenly, 'it was just me being clever. As usual.'

'But when did you write yourself the note?'

'Last night,' he said. 'I saw the scroll at the temple and thought it might be a good idea.'

She sighed. 'I'm guessing we can't go and snatch the scroll now and destroy it instead and stop the whole sorry mess from happening in the first place?'

'The sorry mess that meant we came back in time to be here to be around at the time to stop the whole sorry mess from happening in the first place? Well, we could try that, or we could wait for another day before trying to destroy the universe.'

'I said, I guessed we couldn't do it,' Amy grumbled.

Hetshepsu raised the metal tool and placed it on the coffin's face. 'Awake, Senbeb Nomarch!' he cried. 'May you arise to health, to eat and drink the food we bring, and to join with the gods.'

Amy turned to the Doctor, alarmed. 'What's going on? Some sort of black magic thing?'

'It's called the Opening of the Mouth ceremony,' he told her. 'Symbolically reanimating the dead so they can enjoy the rewards of the afterlife.'

'Phew!' Amy sighed. 'For a moment I thought they were really trying to bring him back to life ag–'

Lady Emu screamed. The coffin lid clattered to the floor, the garlands of flowers bursting apart and sending a rain of scarlet petals over the crowd, making it look like the many white robes were splattered with blood.

The Nomarch was revealed, a bandaged form with a golden painted mask for a face.

The mummy took a step forward. It reached

out with an arm wrapped in bandages and grasped the horrified Hetshepsu by the shoulder as he turned to flee.

Amy thought she would never forget the scream the priest gave. She knew she would never forget the terrified expression on his face as his features crumbled inwards. His wide, frightened eyes collapsed leaving gaping black holes. Worst of all was his mouth, still screaming silently as his lips became paper-thin, teeth bared in an eternal howl.

Then the mummy let go and the skin-covered bones crumpled into a rattling heap.

It happened so quickly. Amy stood frozen, staring, trying to process what she was seeing. He'd been a murderer, he'd tried to kill the Doctor... but to see someone die like that...

Then she saw that Doctor was running forward, of course, and she had to follow. It was a battle to get through the fleeing mourners, all pushing hard in the opposite direction.

Lady Emu had fallen over in the rush and was kneeling on the ground, using her arms and body to shield Nebi and Nubi from the pounding feet. Amy grabbed her arm and pulled her up, the boys with her, tugging them out of the way of the lurching mummy. 'Senbeb, my husband, no...' the scared widow was whispering.

'Come on, let's get you away from here,' said Amy. Lady Emu shrunk away. 'It's me, Amy,' Amy told her, remembering she was in disguise. 'I'm going to get you out of this. Trust me.' The crowd was still milling around in terror and she couldn't see a way out, so she put her head down and charged, pulling Lady Emu and the children with her. Her ankle-length skirt made speed impossible so she ripped it up the side in order to run more freely.

It was quieter now, the fleeing crowd too breathless to scream. Desert sand flew in a storm around the runners, making them cough and choke. Amy stopped for a moment to look back, hoping to see the Doctor, but the clouds of sand were denser than fog and she had no idea where he was now – no idea where the mummy was, either.

They were just following the crowd, but it seemed to be making for the city. 'Home! I want to go home!' Lady Emu cried.

'We'll get you there,' Amy said determinedly.

They were nearly at the edge of the desert now. Nebi and Nubi were slowing, exhausted from their flight, so Amy and Lady Emu picked up a child each and kept running. They crossed the city limits and the crowd began to thin out, each person making for their own part of town. Finally Amy stopped, and to her own surprise she found herself laughing, almost hysterically.

'What amuses you so?!' asked Emu, her voice almost hysterical too.

Amy gulped air in through her laughter. 'I'm not sure! Oh, yes I am. In every mummy movie I've ever seen I've shouted at the screen, "Why are you running? It's walking far too slowly to ever catch you!" And now here I am in a real-life mummy movie and I'm running like a mad thing.' She gave a big sigh. 'And you're looking at me like I'm a mad thing. Never mind. Come on. I'll walk you back home – walk, note – and then I'll go back and find the Doctor.'

Suddenly the screaming started again – but now it was coming from in front of them. From the direction of the market place.

'Oh no,' said Amy. 'Look, you can get back to the palace on your own. I'd better see what's happening.'

Not waiting to see if Lady Emu agreed, Amy sprinted off again. At the edge of the market square, she skidded to a halt, feeling a bit sick.

No, feeling very sick.

Bodies lay everywhere. Twisted, drained, skeletal bodies. And stalking among the litter of bony corpses were others of the same, their stick arms held out in front of them, shrivelled fingers grasping ceaselessly. Amy thought she recognised the original occupants of the now-empty plinth, and she suddenly realised with horror why one of the mummies had disappeared earlier – and why a new withered body had been found.

But there was something else, something worse.

She'd looked at those mummies for a long time, their shrunken features imprinted on her brain. But now...

They were a tiny bit fatter. A tiny bit less emaciated. A tiny bit more bloated.

Amy worked it out in an instant. They were draining the water from every living thing they touched, and taking it into themselves.

And to her eyes, it looked as though their skin had taken on the faintest hue of purple...

CHAPTER 14

MUMMIES, ZOMBIES AND CROCS

Amy realised there was nothing she could do there. No one needed her to tell them to keep out of the way of the mummies, they were doing that all by themselves. Best thing she could do would be to find the Doctor, let him know what was happening.

She was on her way back to the desert when she spotted Khenti. He was limping badly, and she veered in his direction. 'You all right?' she said, noticing there were smears of blood on his face too.

He nodded. 'Just caught in the crush. Have you seen the Lady Emu?'

'Should be back at the palace by now.' Amy went to move off again, but Khenti was looking so exhausted and unhappy that she turned back and took his arm. 'Come on, lean on me. I'll help you there.'

'The Lord Senbeb is angry,' Khenti said, almost to himself, as he hobbled along beside her. 'He knows that I embraced his lady. I have brought this upon our city.'

'Don't be a silly goose,' said Amy. 'It's all a lot more complicated – or possibly a lot more simple, I'm not sure – than that. And decidedly more alien, I'm guessing. Anyway, the point is, it's not your fault.'

They reached the courtyard. The Doctor's moat was still pooling water around the purple reeds and Amy was pleased to note they hadn't spread out any further. She led Khenti to the main door. 'Here you go,' she said. 'You'll be all right from here – what is that?!'

Something was shuffling towards them, a long, toothy creature mottled orange and grey and mauve, looking like some bizarre bruised fossil.

'The crocodile – it is the crocodile!' cried Khenti, and Amy realised he was right, recognising the creepy mummified creature he'd shown her earlier.

They backed away. It was a slow moving thing, Amy didn't exactly feel in any danger, but the sight of the crawling monster almost hypnotised her. She couldn't stop looking at it.

'Move!' Khenti hissed at her. 'Get out of its way!'

With a start Amy moved out of the crocodile's path. She'd expected it to follow her, but it didn't. The beast kept on a straight path, heading for the fish pond.

'It's going to fall in,' Khenti said. 'Do we – do we try to stop it?'

Amy shook her head. 'The water's attracting it. Let it go.'

They watched from a safe distance as the crocodile dragged itself forward. It reached the Doctor's moat but kept going, uprooted papyri clinging to its skin. It passed the edge of the pond and still didn't stop, its front legs waving uselessly in the air until it overbalanced and tipped downwards into the water.

Amy and Khenti followed it to the pond. They hung over the edge and watched.

'It's getting bigger,' said Khenti after a moment.

'Yes – no,' said Amy, observing the crocodile carefully. 'It's just swelling up. It's absorbing water.'

'But it's bigger now than it would have been alive!' Khenti pointed out.

Amy realised he was right. 'It can't stop taking in water!'

'I have seen this with insects,' said Khenti. 'They come to suck your blood, but find they cannot detach themselves. They take in more and more blood, until finally...'

'They burst!' completed Amy. 'Quick! Get back! Get back!'

She grabbed Khenti's arm, tugging him backwards. He stumbled on his injured leg and they both ended up face down on the ground.

From behind them came an extremely wet-sounding crump. Something could be heard splattering down to their rear. 'Ugh,' said Amy as she pulled herself to her feet. 'That is one of the most disgusting things I have ever seen.'

She helped Khenti to stand and they surveyed the courtyard. Lumps of soggy crocodile were plastered over the tiles.

'It is not a pleasant sight,' the scribe agreed. He started to lean down to look at the remains more closely, but Amy held him back. 'Don't touch,' she said. 'We don't know what sort of powers this stuff has. If I were you, I'd get it all cleaned up – now – but for goodness' sake don't let anyone touch it. Just in case.'

Khenti nodded. 'I will do as you say. But you – what are you going to do?'

'I'm off to find the Doctor. He'll want to know about this. I just hope...' She didn't complete the sentence. There were so many things she hoped for.

The silence in the ruined palace was disturbing. No wind blew outside, and Rory hadn't heard the sound of a bird or animal since they arrived. By now, people were barely speaking. So when the noise came, everyone looked up.

A rustling, swishing sound. Someone – or something – was coming towards them from outside.

'It's the Doctor!' Rory cried in relief. He couldn't see anything or anyone, just the forest of purple that surrounded them, but who else could it be? The Doctor would come striding into the palace, dressed in some incredible spacesuit to protect him from the plants. The ordeal was over.

The ordeal wasn't over, and it wasn't the Doctor. Rory watched in horror as the reeds parted to let through an ambling scarecrow form. He didn't recognise it – no one could have recognised it – but he thought he recognised the clothes.

Others recognised them too. 'Yafeu! Yafeu has returned!' One man ran forward, whether to greet or confront his one-time colleague, Rory didn't know.

'Stop!' Rory shouted, and to his relief the man

halted at the edge of the stone floor. Because Rory had seen that Yafeu was not alone. Other stick-thin zombies were also shuffling towards the ruin. One looked to Rory like the cook, Gahiji, the papyrus's first victim.

The workers were running back, trying to get out of the mummies' path – all except the man who had run towards Yafeu. He was still perched at the edge of the building, staring at the oncoming creatures in horror, seemingly unable to move. Rory tried to get towards him, but was crushed in the crowd of panicking Egyptians.

As Yafeu reached the ruin, the man finally tried to run. It was far too late. A withered hand reached out and grasped him. He screamed.

Rory was still trying to push through the hordes of workers; he didn't see exactly what happened. But he could imagine it. And the mummies moved closer and closer...

The Doctor was as surprised as anyone when the Nomarch's mummy burst out of its coffin. He tried to work it out as he ran towards the trouble, discarding the Anubis helmet as he went – spores, perhaps, spores from the plant pass to the victim while it's draining the fluid. Spores infect the host, making it as desperate for water as its attacker, just as the reeds spread and move out in search of water, so the new host searches for water. Its articulated structure means the host can be made to move more effectively...

Yes. So although the host mummy had been reanimated, there was no spark of intelligence there. This shuffling creature bore no resemblance to the person it had once been; it was just a collection of impulses that had taken root in a human form. The Doctor need have no qualms about dealing with it.

If he could deal with it, of course. Best not to just assume...

Around him, people were fleeing. He saw Lady Emu stumble, but also saw Amy pick her up and lead her and her children away, so he knew he didn't have to worry about any of them as the mummy kept striding forward.

The Nomarch had been a large man, and he'd been wrapped in an enormous quantity of linen. But, thought the Doctor, however fearsome the mummy seemed, it was really only skin and bone and cloth. Not particularly substantial. He hefted one of the pomegranates he was carrying. 'I used to be quite good with a cricket ball...' he said aloud. 'Sorry, Senbeb. You don't have a lot of luck with pomegranates, do you? Howzat!' The pomegranate hit the mummy in the centre of its chest and it wobbled for a moment, off balance. The Doctor grabbed another and threw again. The mummy staggered backwards.

It took three more pomegranates to knock it on to the floor. Even then its limbs kept moving, trying to propel it towards anything that might be a source of water. The Doctor looked at it for a few seconds, wondering how much danger it still posed. Probably quite a bit, he decided.

Hetshepsu's adze – the ceremonial tool – was lying by the ex-priest. The Doctor picked it up and stuck it through the mummy's bandages, using it like a tent peg to pin the cloth to the ground. The mummy began pulling like a dog on a lead, and the Doctor knew the axe-like tool wouldn't hold it down for long.

Suddenly, however, the mummy gave a final shudder and lay still. Surprised, the Doctor crept closer to make sure the threat was over.

Something was wriggling like worms beneath the bandages. Something that was trying to break free.

Purple shoots burst through the linen, some upwards towards the light, others going downwards to root themselves in the desert sand. The Doctor stumbled back so the fronds wouldn't touch him. But he knew he wasn't safe for long. In the dry desert, the reeds would start to spread out further and further in search of water, just as they had done in the future. At least here in the past the river was full – almost too full – and the reeds might stop when they reached it. But what harm might they do in the meantime...?

He'd better go and find Amy.

He set off – and then after a few steps came running hurriedly back. He snatched up the fallen Book of the Dead and unrolled it. "Dear Doctor," he read, "here are the coordinates you need, love from the Doctor". Old High Gallifreyan. No one on Earth would be able to read it. Hetshepsu had probably thought it was some elaborate decoration. But two days ago and in two thousand years time, it would bring the TARDIS here.

Having found his prize, the Doctor headed off again – but not towards the city, further out into the desert. He had to make sure the scroll ended up in a safe place – a place where the waters of the Nile would never reach – so it could be dug up again, far in the future, by Grenfell and Hunt.

His task complete, he approached the city once more. He came across people who had been injured in the rush from the funeral parade. The Doctor helped up the fallen and sent them on their way. They clung on to each other for support. One man was lying unconscious, and when the Doctor tried to roll him over on his back he discovered it was Manu, the embalmer. Manu was heavy, but the Doctor managed to pull him up and get him across his shoulders in a fireman's lift. Bearing his burden, he staggered off towards the city, to find Amy. There were an awful lot of problems to deal with here, but he'd just have to cope with them one at a time.

CHAPTER 15

LET IT FLOOD

As it turned out, it was Amy who found the Doctor. The Doctor laid Manu on the sand and he and Amy quickly began to swap news. The Doctor was not at all happy to learn that there were more mobile mummies around. In turn, Amy was shocked to know that the mummies might eventually start to sprout alien reeds.

'Maybe we could fashion some sort of digger,' the Doctor mused. 'They might be clinging tight to the soil – or sand – to get water from its depths, but if we could somehow get deep enough we could uproot them.'

Amy frowned. 'Hang on, the crocodile – I

haven't told you about the crocodile, have I?' She explained about the mummified animal exploding in the water.

By the time she had finished, the Doctor's eyes were glowing. He grabbed Amy's arms and began to dance her round and round, laughing out loud. 'Er, have you gone a bit mad?' she asked, laughing too. 'Or is this some sort of Time Lord "I laugh in the face of danger" bravado thing?'

'Neither!' he cried. 'Well, maybe the mad one a bit. But this is pure, sincere, I-have-solved-everyone's-problems laughter!'

'Well, good,' she said. 'That's nice. How?'

He stopped swinging her round. 'Water. I am going to steal some water to catch the Water Thief.'

Amy had insisted she was coming with the Doctor to help. He had been just as firm that someone had to go back to the city to warn them what was about to happen. Luckily for Amy, Manu had recovered consciousness before the argument got too heated, and the rather confused embalmer had been dispatched on the errand instead. 'Just find Khenti or Lady Emu,' Amy had told him. 'They'll sort it all out if you can just explain what we need.'

'But what you say is impossible!' Manu protested. 'Men cannot control the Nile!'

'So who can control it?' said the Doctor patiently.

'Only the gods,' was the answer.

'And who is your living god here in Egypt?'

'The great pharaoh, of course.'

'And who do we come from?'

Manu's eyes widened. 'You mean...'

'That's right,' said the Doctor. 'We'll have a word with the pharaoh, he'll have a word with the rest of the gods, get them to send the flood early. Nothing easier.' He dropped his light tone and stared Manu straight in the eye. 'Manu, I'm serious. This is going to happen. I'm relying on you to make sure everyone stays safe.'

'You can rely on me, oh Lord Doctor!' Manu cried eagerly. 'Thank you for bestowing this honour upon me.'

'Oh, and say goodbye to everyone from me,' Amy had called as Manu hurried off. 'We're probably not coming back...'

Now she and the Doctor were on their way back to the TARDIS.

'Is this really going to work?' Amy asked.

'Of course it is,' said the Doctor. 'Have you ever known any of my plans fail?'

'Yes,' said Amy. 'There was –'

'OK, OK, OK.' The Doctor interrupted her before she could start on a list. 'The point is, this one won't. Probably. Look, you've discovered that although the mummies are as desperate for water as the plants, they're not built to take it. Dunk a mummy in enough water and it'll explode.'

'Well, the crocodile did,' said Amy. 'We've just got to hope it's the same for all of them.'

'No reason why not,' said the Doctor. 'Now, that would still leave us with the purple papyri to deal with, but we know that reeds are not only safer if they've got a good water supply, they can also be easily uprooted. If the city gets flooded, all our problems get solved at once. The mummies go pop, the reeds get swept up in the flow and we're able to pick them up and deal with them at our leisure.'

'So we're going to go up these mountains and, what, use a hairdryer on them?'

'Something like that,' the Doctor agreed.

Amy tried to dredge every last scrap of information she'd learned about inundation from the corners of her memory. The Nile flooded every year on to the Black Land – so called because of the fertile silt left behind when the water receded, the substance that enabled them to grow crops. Some years the Nile didn't flood enough and some of the land remained infertile. Other years it flooded too much and buildings were washed away. The Egyptians believed that the gods sent the flood, but it was really caused by the warmer summer weather melting the snow on the mountains of Ethiopia, which joined with heavy summer rains to provide more water than the Nile could take.

Now the Doctor was aiming to bring the flood a little early.

'We won't land,' he explained. 'Just hover a bit. Extend out the TARDIS forcefield and agitate the particles a bit so it gets warm. Lot of snowmelt, rushing down. Then we go back to Oxyrhynchus. A few nudges with the forcefield as soon as Khenti and Lady Emu have got the place evacuated, then the water sweeps through. By the time it gets here it'll be powerful enough to take all the plants with it. Then...'

'Yes, that's the bit I'm really worried about,' said Amy. 'It sounds a bit – complicated.'

'Trust me,' said the Doctor.

Amy sighed.

Amy had to admit that the plan was working – so far. The TARDIS was hovering above the city, and the waters were flooding through. 'You wanted to be by the seaside!' the Doctor yelled above the roaring river.

'I'm not going paddling in this!' Amy shouted back. 'And I haven't spotted a single ice cream shop either.' What she had spotted was the bandaged form of the Nomarch's mummy being tossed along by the waves.' She called over her shoulder, 'Hadn't we better get going with the next bit of your marvellous plan? Or the water's going to carry those deadly plants over the whole of the Nile valley.'

The Doctor started operating controls, his fingers dancing around the console. 'Try to be a bit patient, will you, I've never done this before.'

'Now you tell me...' Amy muttered under her breath.

'There!' The Doctor hit a final button and sprang back. He joined her at the open doors, looking out over the churning waters. 'Force field scoop – activated!'

It was an astonishing sight. The water below stopped flowing outwards and started flowing up! Like a backwards tidal wave it came higher and higher until it was no longer touching the ground at all, a vast ball of blue suspended in the air below the TARDIS.

'Hang on a minute,' said Amy, 'you didn't

actually mention what you were going to do next. What can we do with a million trillion gallons of water?'

The Doctor grinned. 'I'm planning to kill two purple birds with one watery stone...'

Rory and the others were huddled in the centre of the ruin, a huge mass of scared men standing back to back. The mummies were surrounding them, moving in.

'Come on, Doctor,' Rory muttered. 'Now would be a really good time to turn up...' He turned to the archaeologists. 'If only we had some water,' he said. 'Something to distract them.'

Hunt's eyes lit up. 'No water any more... but we have its opposite.' He drew a bundle of matches from his pocket. 'Those things are dry as tinder. They'll burn.'

'Are you sure it'll be safe?' Rory said. As a nurse he'd seen the victims of too many accidents to be complacent about fire.

Hunt shrugged. 'We'll just have to pray. Any

attempt is better than the alternative.'

They searched through pockets, finding anything that might be combustible. Darting out from the circle, Rory and the two archaeologists threw screwed up papers in the mummies' paths, then tossed on a lit match...

As each mummy reached the burning litter, there was a whoosh of flame. The cowering men in the centre of the room suddenly found themselves enclosed in a circle of fire. 'This isn't good!' Rory shouted.

And then the skies opened.

'Rory! Rory!' Amy screamed. 'Catch!'

She threw a lifebelt into the churning waters below. During their short journey in the Vortex she'd collected up anything she could find that would float, from lifebelts (rather worryingly labelled *SS Mary Celeste*) to inflatable ducks to armbands and floats in the shape of whales and even a rubber dinghy. As soon as they materialised – in exactly the same spot from which they'd dematerialised thousands of years earlier – the Doctor had released the force field scoop that was holding up the water. (He told Amy as he was doing it that he really hadn't been sure it would hold during the trip through the Vortex, and was fairly surprised to discover his plan had worked.)

Now the Nile waters of long ago were sweeping through Oxyrhynchus once again, extinguishing the flames that had been threatening the palace and taking with them the reeds, the mummies, and everything else that wasn't glued down – which included Rory.

Rory caught the lifebelt just as the giant wave caught him. He had no control over his fate, all he could do was cling tightly to the red-and-white ring. A mummy floated past him – or at least what had once been a mummy, it was now bloating up like an overfilled balloon. And just as he made the comparison, the mummy, like a balloon, burst into bits.

And then, just as Rory was wondering if he

would be carried all the way to the Mediterranean, the water calmed down. He stared around, trying to work out where he was, trying to work out if Grenfell and Hunt and all the other men were there too. He spotted Hunt, who was holding on to an inflatable ring with a swan's head on it, and swam towards him. The archaeologist seemed slightly dazed, but happy and amazed at the same time. 'I don't believe it!' he cried. 'We're in the river! The waters have filled the river!'

Rory realised the man was right. The flood had found its natural home – it had drained into the dried-out river bed. And here, landing on the bank beside him, was the TARDIS. Amy waved from the open door.

'Am I pleased to see you,' Rory said, paddling towards the edge of the river.

'I'm a bit pleased to see you too,' said Amy, giving him a kiss as he climbed up on the bank. 'Now, how d'you feel about helping us collect all those reeds...?'

CHAPTER 16
THE WATER HUNTER

The flood hadn't reached the precious rubbish heaps in the desert, and the town and camp were a little damp but no more worse for wear than that. Even the papyrus documents had kept perfectly safe and dry inside their biscuit tins. The 'Water Thief' reeds, loosened at their roots by the water, were collected up with the help of some giant fishing nets from the TARDIS – which the Doctor, not wanting to explain in too much detail, claimed he had found "just lying around". He also claimed to have found a dozen fruit cakes, twenty entire Edam cheeses and eighteen crates of bananas "just lying around", which was even less plausible – but

Grenfell, Hunt and the Egyptians were too hungry to ask many questions. While the archaeologists and their team were feasting, the Doctor, Rory and Amy hurried back to the TARDIS. Well, the Doctor and Amy hurried, half dragging a reluctant Rory, who'd been about to take a bite of fruit cake.

'I haven't eaten since the day before yesterday!' he said.

'Well, I haven't eaten since something or other BC, but you don't hear me complaining!' said Amy, but gave him a big kiss. 'Didn't mean it, silly. Come on, I've made us a picnic.'

They ate their picnic by the sea. 'At least we've got our seaside holiday at last,' said Amy, munching a stick of celery. 'Even if we had to jump through a few hoops to get here. This is perfect. Sun, sand, sandwiches, no crowds, and a lot of sea.'

'Ninety-nine per cent of the planet's water, the Doctor said,' Rory confirmed. 'And uninhabited, so no one'll be in danger even if the papyri suck the world dry.'

'The purple papyrus's perfect planet,' said Amy.

Rory gazed out across the endless sea, where a small speck was rapidly turning into the Doctor in a dinghy. 'Funny, that. Yesterday I'd have given my right arm for a glass of water, now here's a planetful and I'm rapidly getting sick of the sight of it.'

Amy shrugged. 'We can go as soon as the Doctor's got rid of the reeds. I think that was the last lot.'

'I wonder where they came from in the first place,' Rory said with a frown. 'And how they got to Earth. I know it doesn't really matter now the Doctor's sorted everything out, but it'd be interesting to know.'

'Yeah, like it'd mean anything if we did know,' said Amy dismissively. 'Ooh, purple reeds from the planet Purplereedia fell through space; we'll never have heard of wherever they come from anyway.'

'Oh yes you would,' said the Doctor, as he pulled the rubber dinghy to shore nearby. 'They came from a little planet we all know rather well called Earth.'

'No way!' said Amy. 'You mean they were native plants?'

The Doctor shook his head. 'Not to that time. Looked it up in the TARDIS databanks earlier, while you were searching for your sun cream. It's a genetically engineered crop from the twenty-seventh century, developed specifically to grow in desert regions. And d'you know what they called it? The water hunter. Not thief, hunter. Hunters provide, thieves take. It was meant for good.'

'But how did it get back to Ancient Egypt?' Rory asked.

'Oh, who can tell? Time storm, time path, a few spores carried on the coat of a time traveller, a seed pod stuck in a crevice of a TARDIS...'

Amy almost shrieked. 'It couldn't've been us, though, could it? The seedpod arrived in the past before we did!'

'Not us, not this time,' the Doctor assured her. 'But I've been to Egypt before. I've been to the twenty-seventh century before. I can't be sure it wasn't me.'

'People died,' said Amy. 'The Nomarch, those thieves, other people whose names I don't know. The cook at the dig. Even that horrible ol' Hetshepsu wouldn't have died if it hadn't been for the reeds. He might not have become a murderer in the first place. His heart might have weighed lighter than a feather. Maybe this time travel lark isn't all it's cracked up to be.'

The Doctor was silent. It was Rory who answered, eventually. 'We can't think like that,' he said. 'The Doctor's done so much good, Amy. We've done so much good. Sometimes bad things might happen too, but all we can do is try to be as careful as possible. If we sat at home all day, never going anywhere, never doing anything – well, we'd never do any harm, but we'd never do any good either. We always act for the best. You know that.'

'The road to the underworld is paved with good intentions,' muttered the Doctor. 'But Ammit's never going to get my hearts...'

'What?' asked Rory, puzzled.

The Doctor just said, 'Finished your picnic?'

'Yup. I'm stuffed,' said Rory.

'Ready to go then?'

'Yes,' said both Amy and Rory.

They had to try to make the universe a better place. They didn't need the threat of a crocodile-lion-hippo thing waiting for them at the end. Wherever they might end up, Amy knew that Rory had a point. They would do the right thing. Just because it was the right thing to do.

THE END

DOCTOR WHO

The journey through time and space never ends...
For more exciting adventures, look out for

DOCTOR WHO

The journey through time and space never ends...
For more exciting adventures, look out for

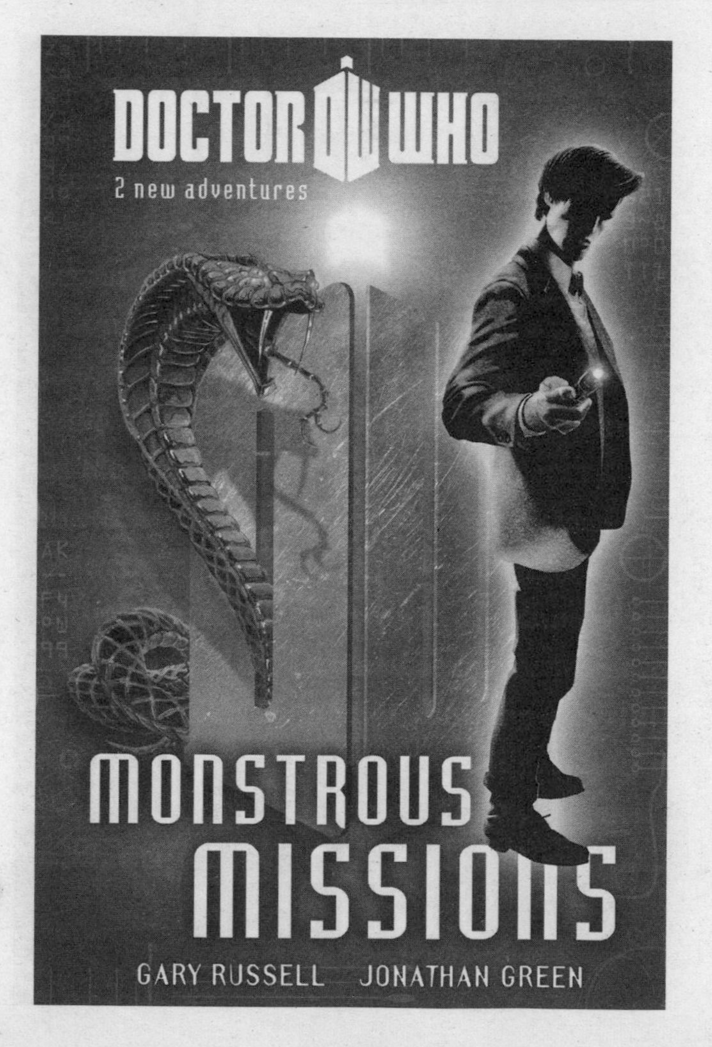